T0311276

The Annotated Importance of Being Earnest

The Annotated Importance of Being Earnest

Oscar Wilde

Edited by Nicholas Frankel

Harvard University Press

CAMBRIDGE, MASSACHUSETTS

LONDON, ENGLAND ⸙ 2015

Library of Congress Cataloging-in-Publication Data
Wilde, Oscar, 1854–1900.
    The Annotated Importance of Being Earnest / Oscar Wilde ;
edited by Nicholas Frankel.
        pages cm
    ISBN 978-0-674-04898-0 (alk. paper)
    1. Identity (Psychology)—Drama.   2. Foundlings—Drama.
3. England—Drama.   4. Comedies.   I. Frankel, Nicholas,
1962– editor.   II. Title.
    PR5818.I4 2015
    822'.8—dc23   2014034673

Book designed by Dean Bornstein

Contents

Preface

"The truth is rarely pure and never simple," declares Algernon early in Act 1 of *The Importance of Being Earnest,* and were it either, "modern literature [would be] a complete impossibility." *The Importance of Being Earnest* is itself an example of the kind of complex, modern, literary work Algernon has in mind. It is full of subtexts, disguises, concealments, and double entendres. Even names are not what they seem. When Ernest is unmasked as plain Jack or John, we delight in a brief slipping of the veil, as well as in the promised resolution of the complications that stem from the lies he has spun. But we delight even more in those very complications—it is the business of art to tell lies, Wilde tells us in "The Decay of Lying"—and it is only a matter of time before Jack will be restored to his "true" self as Ernest.

The Importance of Being Earnest requires careful explication and annotation because it means much more than it says. All art is at once surface and symbol, Wilde tells us in his preface to *The Picture of Dorian Gray,* but "those who go beneath the surface do so at their peril." Just how perilous that venture was for Wilde's contemporaries has only recently become fully clear to us, as we begin to understand the commercial, social, and legal imperatives that forced Wilde beneath the surface. In the present edition of *The Importance of Being Earnest*, I continue the work I began in *The Picture of Dorian Gray: An Annotated, Uncensored Edition* (2011), as well as *The Uncensored Picture of Dorian Gray* (2012). Virtually from the moment Wilde abandoned a promising career in journalism to become a writer of fiction and drama, he began to play a cat-and-mouse game of revealing and concealing his sexual identity in his published works. But never were the stakes higher than in 1895, when *The Importance of Being Earnest* was first produced and when Wilde was to be imprisoned for "gross indecency." Wilde had only narrowly escaped prosecution in 1890 for the publication of *Dorian Gray* (the novel was nevertheless used against him in court in 1895), while his play *Salomé* had been refused a performance license by the Censor in 1892. The legal climate was hostile, and as the censorship of *Dorian Gray* indicates, it was imperative that Wilde mask his meanings behind words that seem pure and simple.

The introduction that follows demonstrates how and why *The Importance of Being Earnest* cleaves closely to its author's sexual identity. In the annotations that accompany the text, I have illuminated biographical allusions that either Wilde deliberately veiled or that have become clear only with the passing of time. Nonetheless, other principles have also guided my annotations: like many works of Victorian literature, the play is deeply rooted in its original historical moment, and Wilde's references to "The Albany," "Willis's," "Liberal Unionist," and the like, which his early audiences would have understood with ease, require explanation for a modern readership. I have also pointed up the play's relations with other works by Wilde, whose oeuvre is more intellectually unified and less piecemeal than is often held to be the case. Finally, in calling attention to the large amount of material that was incorporated shortly before the play's publication in 1899, four years after it was first performed, I have thrown into relief the large and telling gap between the play's witty veneer and the circumstances faced by its author—an impoverished, exiled sex criminal—at the moment of its original publication.

My intention throughout has been to enlarge the understanding and pleasure of twenty-first-century readers; and to the extent that I have succeeded, this edition will interest general readers and those with little prior knowledge of Wilde's play, as well as teachers, students, scholars, directors, dramaturges, and others with a more specialized interest in Wilde's play. The work of previous editors constitutes the foundation on which I have built, and my debts to them, especially Joseph Donohue and Russell Jackson, will be evident in my notes.

A Note on the Text

The Importance of Being Earnest was originally drafted as a four-act play in 1894. During rehearsals for the play's first production at London's St. James's Theatre in 1895, the actor-manager George Alexander asked Wilde to cut the play to a more manageable three acts and make other significant changes. It is not uncommon in the life of a play that the first production serves as a kind of workshop, in which the original draft becomes transformed by the demands of theatrical performance. The present text is based on the first and only edition of *The Importance of Being Earnest* to appear in Wilde's lifetime, published by Leonard Smithers in February 1899. Wilde himself shepherded the play into print. Living in exile and near poverty in Paris at the time, he arranged for the text used in the St. James's production to be typed up and sent to him before sitting down to revise the play.

In preparing the play for publication, Wilde added many witticisms, sharpened dialogue, altered stage directions, and made numerous other changes. Some of the play's most memorable lines—"The good end happily, and the bad unhappily. That is what Fiction means," "If I am occasionally a little over-dressed, I make up for it by being always immensely over-educated," "in England . . . education produces no effect whatsoever, [although] if it did, it would prove a serious danger to the upper classes"—were not introduced until Wilde's revision in 1899. The annotations in the present edition call attention to these and other significant changes made by Wilde.

For Wilde, as for other playwrights of the 1890s (George Bernard Shaw, Arthur Wing Pinero, Henry Arthur Jones), a play's publication was a sign of its status as literature. *The Importance of Being Earnest* should be "identical . . . with the format of [my] other plays," Wilde insisted to his publisher, and it should have "a similar cover, same cloth, same colour, and similar design." By virtue of the care with which Wilde attended to every aspect of its original publication in 1899, the present text is the swiftest, wittiest, and final embodiment of *The Importance of Being Earnest* descending from its author's lifetime, and it has the clear authority of an edition prepared in accordance with its author's wishes.

The Annotated Importance of Being Earnest

The St. James's Theatre, c. 1895.
Photo by Alfred Ellis, from *Round London: an album of pictures from photographs of the chief places of interest in and round London* (London: G. Newnes, 1896). Alderman Library, University of Virginia.

Introduction

On the evening of the premiere of *The Importance of Being Earnest*, St. Valentine's Day in 1895, at London's St. James's Theatre, the weather could not have been more foreboding. "There was a snow-storm more severe than had been remembered in London for years," Wilde's friend Ada Leverson later recalled, and "a black, bitter, threatening wind blew the drifting snow."[1] Dressed to the hilt for the occasion, the fashionable first-night audience was undeterred. The opening of Wilde's new play—his fourth in London's West End in only three years—was a major social event. Although rumors had been circulating about Wilde's intimacies with a string of young men—especially with Lord Alfred Douglas, the youngest son of the Marquess of Queensberry—Wilde had long been the main attraction at London salons, artistic at-homes, and exclusive dinner parties.[2] Having a ticket to the first night of a new play by Wilde suggested taste and social distinction. The St. James's Theatre, moreover, had a reputation as London's most distinguished and literary theater—it specialized in Society Drama, fashionable modern plays in which the rarified world of the English upper classes was held up for conscious dramatic inspection—and London Society was out in force on this cold, wintry night. "Most of the smart young men held tall canes of ebony with ivory tops," Leverson later reflected; they wore "white gloves with rows of black stitching and very pointed shoes" and "buttonholes of the delicate bloom or lily-of-the-valley," while "nearly all the pretty women wore sprays of lilies against their large puffed sleeves": it was an audience "such as is rarely seen nowadays either at the Opera or even at a first night of a Russian Ballet."[3]

Wilde's play announced itself as "a trivial comedy for serious people" (the subtitle, printed in programs and playbills, was altered at the last moment during rehearsals from "a serious comedy for trivial people"). Whether or not this backhanded witticism amused the first-night audience, they laughed uproariously throughout the performance, in which they saw themselves reflected in the mirror the play held up to the late-Victorian elite. *The Importance of Being Earnest* quickly came to be seen as Wilde's greatest theatrical triumph. " 'Farce' is far too gross and commonplace a word to apply to such an iridescent filament of fantasy," declared the critic William Archer, the champion of Henrik Ibsen: Wilde takes commonplace theatrical conventions and with great humor "transmutes them into something entirely new and individual," revealing himself to be a "born playwright."[4] "Oscar Wilde may be said to have at last, and by a single stroke, put his enemies under his feet," proclaimed the *New York Times:* "Their name is legion, but the most inveterate of them may be defied to go to the St. James's Theatre and keep a straight face through the performance of *The Importance of Being Earnest.* It is a pure farce . . . loaded with drolleries, epigrams, impertinences, and bubbling comicalities. . . . I have not heard such unrestrained, incessant laughter from all parts of the theatre, and those laughed the loudest whose approved mission it is to read Oscar long lectures . . . on his dramatic and ethical shortcomings. The thing is as slight in structure and as

· devoid of purpose as a paper balloon, but it is extraordinarily funny, and the universal assumption is that it will remain on the boards here for an indefinitely extended period."[5]

Wilde's triumph was short-lived. While the *Times*'s correspondent was right about the play's merits, his prediction of milestone success could not have been more wrong. What neither he nor the play's producers foresaw was the series of scandalous trials that would become a *cause célèbre* as the details of Wilde's secret double life were made public. In an extraordinary reversal of fortune, England's most feted playwright and colorful personality was about to become its most notorious sexual criminal. Within two months, following Wilde's arrest on 5 April 1895 for the crime of "gross indecency," Wilde's name was removed from both the programs and the posters outside the St. James's Theatre; and then, on 8 May, a day after his release from remand prison on bail, while Wilde anxiously awaited the commencement of his second criminal trial (the first had ended inconclusively a week earlier, with a hung jury), the play closed for good after eighty-three performances.[6] In removing Wilde's name from printed materials,[7] the play's producers were trying to dissociate themselves and the production from Wilde's disgrace; but audiences continued avoiding the St. James's Theatre over the ensuing weeks, and the few who ventured into the mostly empty auditorium "saw [the play] with a sense of oppression."[8] The producers' ill-conceived strategy had backfired: it only stirred further panic and contempt. Even those who were loyal to Wilde, such as the American actor Hermann Vezin, left the theater in disgust: "I'm sorry. I can't stay," Vezin informed his companion shortly after they took their seats and he glanced down at the altered program in his hand, which he then crumpled in anger and

ST. JAMES'S THEATRE.

SOLE LESSEE AND PROPRIETOR . . MR. GEORGE ALEXANDER.

Thursday, February 14th, 1895,

AND EVERY EVENING AT 8.45.

The Importance of being Earnest,

A TRIVIAL COMEDY FOR SERIOUS PEOPLE,

BY OSCAR WILDE.

John Worthing, J.P.	of the Manor House, Woolton, Hertfordshire	Mr. GEORGE ALEXANDER
Algernon Moncrieffe	(his Friend)	Mr. ALLAN AYNESWORTH
Rev. Canon Chasuble, D.D.	(Rector of Woolton)	Mr. H. H. VINCENT
Merriman	(Butler to Mr. Worthing)	Mr. FRANK DYALL
Lane	(Mr. Moncrieffe's Man-servant)	Mr. F. KINSEY PEILE
Lady Bracknell		Miss ROSE LECLERCQ
		(By permission of Mr. J. COMYNS CARR)
Hon. Gwendolen Fairfax	(her Daughter)	Miss IRENE VANBRUGH
Cecily Cardew	(John Worthing's Ward)	Miss EVELYN MILLARD
Miss Prism	(her Governess)	Mrs GEORGE CANNINGE

Time - - The Present.

Act I. - Algernon Moncrieffe's Rooms in Piccadilly (*H. P. Hall*)
Act II. - The Garden at the Manor House, Woolton (*H. P. Hall*)
Act III. - Morning-Room at the Manor House, Woolton (*Walter Hann*)

Preceded, at 8.30, by a Play in One Act. by LANGDON E. MITCHELL, entitled

IN THE SEASON.

Sir Harry Collingwood	Mr. HERBERT WARING
Edward Fairburne	Mr. ARTHUR ROYSTON
Sybil March	Miss ELLIOTT PAGE

Scene - A Room in Sir Harry Collingwood's House.   Time - The Present.

Programme of Music.

MARCH	"Tourniquet"	*Louis Ganne*
FANTASIE	"Pagliacci"	*Leoncavallo*
BOURRÉE	"L'auvergnate"	*Ganne*
MOUVEMENT DE VALSE	"Douce Caresse"	*E. Gillet*
WALZER	"Minnesänger"	*Sabathil*

The Furniture by FRANK GILES & Co., High Street, Kensington.
The Wigs by W. CLARKSON.
The Scenery by H. P. HALL and WALTER HANN.

NO FEES. The Theatre is lighted by Electricity. **NO FEES.**

The Attendants are strictly forbidden to accept gratuities, and are liable to instant dismissal should they do so.
Visitors to the Theatre are earnestly begged to assist the Management in carrying out a regulation framed for their comfort and convenience.

The Etchings and Engravings in the corridors and vestibule supplied and arranged by I. P. MENDOZA, King Street, St. James's.

The Floral Decorations by REID & Co., King Street, St. James's.

Photographs of the Artistes appearing at this Theatre, can be obtained of ALFRED ELLIS, 20, Upper Baker Street, N.W.

FIRST MATINEE SATURDAY, FEBRUARY 23rd, at 3.

PRICES:—Private Boxes, £1 11s. 6d. to £4 4s. Stalls, 10s. 6d. Dress Circle, 7s. Upper Boxes, Numbered and Reserved (Bonnets allowed), 4s. Pit, 2s. 6d. Gallery, 1s.

Box Office (Mr. ARNOLD) open daily from 10 till 5 o'clock, and 8 till 10 p.m.

Seats can be booked one month in advance by Letter or Telegram, or Telephone No. 3903.

Theater program from the opening weeks of the first production, clearly indicating Wilde's authorship of *The Importance of Being Earnest*. Mark Samuels Lasner Collection, on loan to the University of Delaware Library.

revulsion.[9] Vezin was appalled at the producers' bald-faced hypocrisy in wishing to profit from a play whose authorship they refused to acknowledge—to say nothing of the haste and prejudice they exhibited in judging Wilde before he had been tried in a court of justice. "I wonder on what principle of law, or jus-

SOLE LESSEE AND PROPRIETOR - - MR. GEORGE ALEXANDER.

PRODUCED THURSDAY, FEBRUARY 14th. 1895.

Every Evening at 9 (Last Nights)

The Importance of being Earnest,

A TRIVIAL COMEDY FOR SERIOUS PEOPLE.

John Worthing, J.P. { of the Manor House, Woolton, Hertfordshire }		Mr. GEORGE ALEXANDER
Algernon Moncrieffe . (his Friend) .		Mr. ALLAN AYNESWORTH
Rev. Canon Chasuble, D.D. . (Rector of Woolton)		Mr. H. H. VINCENT
Merriman . . (Butler to Mr. Worthing) .		Mr. FRANK DYALL
Lane . . (Mr. Moncrieffe's Man-servant) .		Mr. F. KINSEY PEILE
Lady Bracknell		Mrs. EDWARD SAKER
Hon. Gwendolen Fairfax . (her Daughter) .		Miss IRENE VANBRUGH
Cecily Cardew . (John Worthing's Ward)		Miss EVELYN MILLARD
Miss Prism . . (her Governess) . .		Mrs GEORGE CANNINGE

Time - - The Present.

Act I. - Algernon Moncrieffe's Rooms in Piccadilly (*H. P. Hall*)
Act II. - The Garden at the Manor House, Woolton (*H. P. Hall*)
Act III. - Morning-Room at the Manor House, Woolton (*Walter Hann*)

Preceded, at 8.30, by a Play in One Act, by LANGDON E. MITCHELL. entitled

IN THE SEASON.

Sir Harry Collingwood		Mr. HERBERT WARING
Edward Fairburne . . .		Mr. ARTHUR ROYSTON
Sybil March . . .		Miss ELLIOTT PAGE

Scene - A Room in Sir Harry Collingwood's House. Time - The Present.

Censored theater program (Wilde's name is purged), used during
the last weeks of the first production, printed after Wilde's arrest on
April 5, 1895. Joseph Donohue/Harvard Theater Collection.

tice, or common sense, or good manners, or Christian charity, an author's name is blotted from his work," complained Wilde's fellow playwright Sidney Grundy in a letter to the *Daily Telegraph:* "If a man is not to be credited with what he has done well, by what right is he punished for what he has done ill?"[10] But Vezin and Grundy were in a small minority. Outraged theatergoers stepped up their boycott of the play as the first criminal trial got under way, and then on 25 May, Wilde's downfall was complete when he was found guilty and sentenced to two years' imprisonment with hard labor. It would take another fourteen years before the St. James's Theatre and its lessee, the actor-manager George Alexander, credited Wilde as the play's author.[11]

Within weeks of the play's first performance, then, this "iridescent filament of fantasy" had become indelibly associated with the character of its author, its subversive "trivial comedy" itself subverted by the most personal and serious of tragedies. "It should have been a classic for the English theatre," Wilde later declared, "but alas! the author was struck by madness from the moon."[12] In truth, tragedy and sexual politics are never far from the heart of Wilde's play: Miss Prism, another of the sad Victorian "odd women" whose lives were immortalized in George Gissing's novel of the same title (1893), seems doomed to a spinsterhood, despite the conflicted attentions of the sexless and celibate Canon Chasuble; children are abandoned or treated as commodities by their moneyed, egotistic parents; and the "happy" marriages announced at the play's end threaten to founder on the rocks of mutual deception and miscommunication before they have even begun. "If I ever get married, I shall certainly try to forget the fact," Algernon promises near the play's beginning, and there can be few in the audience who doubt, when the play ends, that Algernon will deliver on this promise. Alone among the first-night critics, George Bernard Shaw found the play "essentially hateful," though he later confessed he had no idea at the time that "Oscar was going to the dogs" or that the play represented "a real degeneracy produced by his debaucheries."[13]

The majority of early reviewers took a somewhat different view of the play, seeing it as an exercise in pure style that would not admit interpretation. They agreed with Archer that the play "imitates nothing, represents nothing, means nothing, [and] is nothing, except a sort of *rondo capriccioso,* in which the artist's fingers run with crisp irresponsibility up and down the keyboard of life." "Why attempt to analyse and class such a play?" asked Archer.[14] One might as well "sit down after dinner and attempt seriously to discuss the true inwardness of a *soufflé,*" declared the reviewer for *Truth.*[15] "In matters of grave importance, style, not sincerity, is the important thing," Gwendolen famously declares in the course of the play. Those in Archer's camp might have said that Shaw was looking for a sincerity the play never possessed—and in the process missing what was most distinctively and brilliantly Wildean about it. As Wilde had coyly asserted in his 1891 preface to *The Picture of Dorian Gray,* "those who go beneath the surface do so at their peril."[16] The play existed to be enjoyed as pure "surface," as a feast of language, wit, and stagecraft. It could be appreciated on aesthetic grounds alone—"the artist is the creator of beautiful things," Wilde declares in his preface—and consequently those, like Shaw, "who find ugly meanings in beautiful things are corrupt without being charming."[17]

The idea that literature is simply a "beautiful thing" was to be put to the severest test in the opening days of April 1895, in the course of Wilde's calamitous legal action against the Marquess of Queensberry, the culminating event in a series of hostilities between Wilde and the father of his lover Lord Alfred Douglas. Queensberry had objected to the friendship between Douglas and the older Wilde almost from its inception in 1892, but from 1894 onward, as the two became inseparable and increasingly careless in their behavior, he threatened Douglas that he would "make a public scandal in a way you little dream of" if Douglas did not end the relationship.[18] In June 1894, taking the matter further, Queensberry appeared unannounced at Wilde's house, accompanied by a prizefighter, and had to be forcibly ejected; and on the opening night of *The Importance of Being Earnest,* Wilde had got wind of, and foiled, an attempt by Queensberry to enter the theater and publicly denounce Wilde from the stage. Four days later, Queensberry, making good on his threat to create a scandal, left a calling card at Wilde's West End club; on the card, he had scrawled, "For Oscar Wilde, posing somdomite" (in haste and in spleen, Queensberry accidentally misspelled "sodomite"), goading Wilde into a libel suit against his nemesis. The collapse of Wilde's libel action—in which it became clear that Wilde had had "indecent" relations with a number of young male prostitutes or "renters" as well as with respectable young men, such as his publisher's clerk Edward Shelley—led directly to Wilde's subsequent arrest and criminal prosecution. "May I take it that no matter how immoral a book was, if it was well-written it would be a good book?" Queensberry's counsel, Edward Carson Q.C., asked Wilde during the libel trial.[19] Carson was attempting to

Oscar Wilde and Lord Alfred Douglas, 1893.
The William Andrews Clark Memorial Library, University of California,
Los Angeles.

prove that Wilde's literary work—in particular, his novel *The Picture of Dorian Gray*—no matter how well written, justified his
client's purportedly libelous scrawl. "If a book is well-written . . . it
produces a sense of beauty," Wilde replied (80), explaining what
he had meant by writing (in the preface to *The Picture of Dorian
Gray*) "There is no such thing as a moral or an immoral book,"
and "books are well written or badly written." So "a well written
book putting forth sodomitical views might be a good book?"
Carson facetiously retorted (80). Although Wilde refuted in court
Carson's implication that his novel "put forth sodomitical views,"
just as he had refuted similar insinuations in the press in 1890,[20]
privately he admitted that his novel "contains much of me in it"
and that he strongly identified with its principal three characters.

For all the play's fame as the epitome of Wildean wit, *The Importance of Being Earnest* also contains much of Wilde in it, and
it is difficult from our twenty-first-century perspective not to see
the play as another coded expression of its author's secret double
life. In early drafts of the play, the dissolute Algernon Moncrieff
is named "Lord Alfred," and he is the son, not the nephew, of
the imperious Lady Bracknell (who is called "Lady Brancaster"
in early drafts of the play). Bracknell, a town in Berkshire, about
thirty miles west of London, was the country home of Lord Alfred Douglas's mother. Wilde's revisions thus move at once in op-
posite directions. While he seems to want to obscure the play's
relation to the real Lord Douglas, he accentuates the biographical connection through the allusion to Douglas's mother—these
"named" coincidences are all the more powerful for the fact that
the play invites us to see personal names as forms of disguise.
Similarly, in the original four-act version of the play that Wilde

wrote and submitted for production, Algernon is at one point served with a writ of attachment (i.e., arrest warrant) for an unpaid debt of over £700 owed to the Savoy Hotel—a writ that Algernon attempts to rebuff by saying, "I always dine at Willis's. It is far more expensive." This plot event dramatically prefigures the writs served on Wilde in the late winter, spring, and summer of 1895 for debts that included £95 (roughly £10,000 or $16,000 in today's money) owed to the Savoy and Willis's for the year 1893 alone, as well as à further £233 for "tobacco, wine, jewelry, flowers, etc."[21] It is also worth noting in this connection that while drafting *The Importance* at Worthing in the late summer of 1894, Wilde was—according to his own 1897 account—besieged with visits from a bored, increasingly reckless Lord Alfred Douglas, who viewed Worthing as "a convenient location for illicit pleasures"[22] and, when Wilde's vacation lease expired, insisted Wilde accompany him to the Metropole Hotel, at Brighton, rather than returning directly to his family in London.[23] Increasingly Wilde was unable to deny Douglas any whim that might be satisfied with money. He even jokingly proposed co-writing, with Douglas, a book to be titled *How to Live above One's Income: For the Use of the Sons of the Rich.*

As one critic has observed, in the early drafts of *The Importance*, Wilde was "sailing perilously close to the wind."[24] Perhaps for this reason, he eliminated the most obvious allusions to his own life before the play was first performed, and they remained invisible to English-language readers and audiences until the 1950s and 1960s, when four-act versions of Wilde's play, based on early drafts, were first published in English.[25] But even so, there is plenty of evidence in the three-act text[26]—which Wilde himself saw through the press in 1899—to suggest that this "trivial comedy" simultaneously reveals and conceals numerous allusions to its author's complex personal life. The most potent evidence is all of the "bunburying" that goes on in the play. The term itself—a witty neologism, based on the name of an invalid friend ("Bunbury") whom Algernon fabricates as a pretext for avoiding social responsibilities and pursuing a secret life of pleasure—has given rise to some interesting and unproven conjectures. Some scholars argue that the name derives from a onetime family friend of Wilde's, named Henry Bunbury, whose only extant letter to Wilde, written in 1878, laments how out of the way and isolated was his own residence in Gloucestershire; others argue that the name was plucked arbitrarily from obscure newspaper obituaries appearing around the time Wilde began composing the play, while still others remind us that—as Wilde (an Irishman) would have been aware—in Gaelic, *bun* means "the bottom or end" of something or even the human posterior.[27] The critic Joel Fineman argues that *bunbury* is a crude and rather obvious pun—that it is "a collection of signifiers that straightforwardly express their desire to bury in the bun."[28] Fineman's suggestion has been contested on the grounds that there exists no evidence that before 1960 or thereabouts the word *bun* was ever used to mean *buttock*.[29] But that is perhaps to underestimate Wilde: a writer of versatile imagination and linguistic ingenuity, Wilde was quite able and willing to invent new puns and double entendres where none previously existed. It has also been proposed—although on the thinnest of evidence—that *bunbury* derives from the obscure village of Bunbury in Cheshire or from an amalgam of two southern English towns, Banbury and Sunbury, commemorating Wilde's furtive meetings at Sunbury with a schoolboy whom he had met when getting into a train at Banbury.[30] Ultimately, the origin of the term is less important than the activity it is intended to describe in the play, since *bunburying* not only means the pursuit of secret and surreptitious pleasures but also suggests a form of behavior or way of life, undertaken with flagrant and self-conscious disregard for social rules and conventions. Following the passage of the 1885 Criminal Law Amendment Act criminalizing "gross indecency" between men, homosexual men were forced to live a secret double life, often requiring elaborate subterfuges. Wilde himself went to considerable pains to disguise from his wife and family the real reasons for his long absences from home—absences spent dining and bedding a series of male sexual partners in London's West End. One scholar even describes the "farcical interludes" in Wilde's family vacation in the summer of 1894—interludes in which Wilde briefly abandoned his family, as well as the composition of *The Importance of Being Earnest*, in order to "amuse himself" with the sixteen-year-old Alphonse Conway, a local boy with whom Wilde became involved sexually after meeting him on the beach at Worthing[31]—as "Bunburying-in-earnest" and "juggling his several lives."[32] So frequently and consistently does Jack *bunbury*, moreover, that the verb spawns its own cognate noun: Algernon calls Jack "a confirmed and secret Bunburyist" and "one of the most advanced Bunburyists I know." Both phrases suggest a secret, private identity, while the term *advanced*, it has recently been suggested, drawn partly from the medical discourse surrounding disease, pathologizes Jack/Ernest, implying that his "Bunburying" is a physical and neurological condition.[33] (In an

influential 1892 critique of "degenerate" culture—in which
Wilde is the target of much venom—the social critic and physician
Max Nordau speaks of "a very advanced state of degeneration" and "an advanced hysteric.")[34] In different and more
serious guises, *bunburying* is to be found, in some form or other,
throughout Wilde's dramatic and fictional works, notably in his
novel *The Picture of Dorian Gray,* in which the eponymous
hero pursues a secret, scandalous, and increasingly reckless life
of pleasure unknown to the world at large. That Wilde himself
was "a confirmed and secret Bunburyist" would be made clear
in the course of the trials.

Another potent piece of evidence is provided by the name "Ernest": the lies and confusions created by Jack and Algernon in
assuming the false name drive the final two acts of the play and
stand behind its punning title. The pun on "earnest" is itself an
ironic reinforcement of the ongoing need for deception. For it is
far more important to be *Ernest.* At the play's conclusion, even
as Jack, newly christened as "Ernest," speaks of "the vital Importance of Being Earnest," the audience understands that he is
incapable of sincerity or conviction, so deep are his devotion to
a world of appearances and his secret enslavement to a world of
pleasure. The Ernest/earnest joke is not, however, Wilde's own
invention. He borrows the pun from an 1892 volume of poems
titled *Love in Earnest* by the homosexual poet John Gambril
Nicholson: in that book, the ballad "Of Boys' Names" ends, "One
name can make my pulses bound, / . . . 'Tis Ernest sets my heart
a-flame." ("Ernest" was in fact the real name of Nicholson's lover.)
By 1895, the name "Ernest" had come to allude to male same-sex
love, at least within a small literary circle.[35] Its use, by Wilde as

by Nicholson before him, made a travesty of the high-Victorian notion of *earnestness,* the belief that a person's identity should be inferred not by actions—always open to interpretation—but by what a person chose to reveal about him- or herself. Earnestness, in this sense, was impossible for homosexuals in the wake of the 1885 Act, and for writers such as Wilde and Nicholson, inverting the common logic of "earnestness" was vital to rearticulating the basis on which male same-sex love was possible. At least two modern scholars, taking their cue from Nicholson, utilize the phrase "love in earnest" to designate male same-sex love.[36]

Another critical allusion to homosexuality and to Wilde's own life lies in the precise location of Jack's (or Ernest's) London residence, "B. 4 The Albany." The Albany was an apartment building just off London's Piccadilly, "planned and built as suites of chambers for the residence of single gentlemen, and named after the Duke of York and Albany, to whom it once belonged."[37] Although the building had once possessed a distinguished reputation (Byron, Gladstone, and Macaulay had all lived there), by Wilde's day, the building "had fallen on difficult times and had acquired a questionable reputation . . . [for] elegance gone to seed and . . . exclusiveness tinged with raciness."[38] That the building shared with nearby Piccadilly a reputation for sexual licentiousness is shown in an early draft of Wilde's play, in which Miss Prism says of Ernest, "I should fancy that he was as bad as any young man who has chambers in the Albany, or indeed in the vicinity of Picadilly [*sic*], can possibly be."[39] But it is not just the Albany's reputation for unspecified sexual raciness that matters in Wilde's allusion, for the precise location of Jack's flat was "E. 4" in the first London and New York productions, deliberately altered to "B. 4" by Wilde as he later prepared the text for publication in 1899. The alteration conceals important personal associations. E. 4 The Albany was the residence of Wilde's friend the homosexual apologist George Ives, later the founder of The Order of Chaeronea, a secret homosexual society established in 1897 in Ives's conviction that homosexuals would never be openly tolerated and therefore must establish a means of underground communication. Jack's residence at E. 4 The Albany is a private joke—one that pokes fun at Ives's elaborate measures for secrecy— and perhaps at Wilde's own anxieties. In 1899, however, following Wilde's conviction and Ives's founding of The Order of Chaeronea, it was not merely diplomatic but also a matter of legal necessity that Wilde should alter "E. 4" to some less incriminating locale within The Albany.

Admittedly these allusions to Wilde's own life would have been invisible to the majority of Wilde's contemporaries, as they remain so today to most audiences, who nonetheless continue to find much to enjoy in the play. In the doubleness and indirectness with which the play spoke of and to homosexual lives, these allusions are the literary equivalent of Ives's Order of Chaeronea, indicating by coded means what could not be openly tolerated or articulated in public. As the critic Regenia Gagnier has remarked, Wilde wrote with a twofold aim—partly to criticize and amuse "an irresponsible mass audience" but also to "create an audience of intimates" who could be expected to appreciate the play at a deeper, more personal level.[40] This coterie would have constituted a small minority on the first night—though it should be remembered that rumors of Wilde's secret vices were entertained or perhaps dismissed by the majority. Almost certainly, many of the personal allusions within *The Importance* were not lost on the players themselves. It is not insignificant that it was actors—specifically Charles Hawtrey and Charles Brookfield, performing in *An Ideal Husband* in London's West End concurrently with the opening run of *The Importance*—who supplied Queensberry's detectives with damaging evidence about Wilde's dalliances with male prostitutes or "renters." When Wilde requested forty stall seats for the opening night of *A Woman of No Importance*, the play's actor-manager Sir Herbert Beerbohm Tree insisted on vetting the names before granting Wilde his wish, leading Wilde in turn to decry what he saw as a personal insult. So far as *The Importance* is concerned, the producer-actor George Alexander, in his role as licensee and manager of the St. James's, was responsible for ejecting Douglas's father, the Marquess of Queensberry, on the opening night, when it was discovered that the Marquess planned to address the audience about Wilde's scandalous dalliance with his youngest son. According to Wilde, "all Scotland Yard—twenty police"—were employed to ensure the Marquess did not gain entry, whereupon the Marquess "prowled about for three hours, then left chattering like a monstrous ape."[41] Before departing, he left a bouquet of rotten vegetables for Wilde at the stage door. If curious theatergoers were unsure about the exact reasons for the large police presence and the Marquess's strange behavior outside the theater, the disturbance would nonetheless have suggested that the border between art and life is easily crossed.

There can be no debate that Wilde himself was deeply conscious of how personal a play *The Importance* was. Reflecting shortly after leaving prison in 1897 on his personal and professional collapse, he confessed, "if I were asked of myself as a dramatist, I would say that my unique position was that I had taken the Drama, the most objective form known to art, and made it as personal a mode of expression as the Lyric or the Sonnet."[42] Wilde does not mean simply that *The Importance* and his other comedies of society were consummate examples of his personal style and wit (though they certainly are that). Rather, by a "personal mode of expression," he means to suggest something more: that he had revealed himself more openly in his plays than most of his contemporaries had realized.

To a certain degree, this element of self-expression was willful and deliberate, part of a dangerous cat-and-mouse game that Wilde had been playing for years in his published works, revealing and concealing himself as an active member of London's homosexual subculture. Wilde had come dangerously close to prosecution for obscenity when publishing his only novel, *The Picture of Dorian Gray*, in the July 1890 number of *Lippincott's Monthly Magazine*. Recognizing that Wilde had gone too far, his editor, J. M. Stoddart, had struck the novel's most graphic homosexual content from Wilde's typescript shortly before publication. Even in its redacted form, the novel caused an uproar in the British press that threatened to ruin Wilde. Among the many vitriolic reactions to the novel, at least two prominent magazines hinted that Wilde and his publishers ought to be prosecuted for what he had written. Foreshadowing by nearly five years the fate that lay in store for Wilde's publications following his conviction, W. H. Smith withdrew the July 1890 number of the magazine from its railway bookstalls, saying that Wilde's story had "been characterized in the press as a filthy one," whereupon the magazine's British copublisher, Ward, Lock & Co., calling W. H. Smith's action a "serious matter," insisted that Wilde incorporate changes into the novel before consenting to publish it in book form.[43]

Chastened by these experiences, Wilde thereafter became more circumspect about revealing himself too openly in his writing. A few weeks before the opening night of *The Importance,* Wilde, determined to conceal elements of the play that related directly to his own life, told an interviewer that his new play was "exquisitely trivial, a delicate bubble of fancy."[44] The interviewer, however, knew better, for he was none other than Wilde's close friend, onetime lover, and later literary executor and editor Robert Baldwin Ross. Wilde had in fact put many elements of his personal life in the play. In *The Importance,* and in much of Wilde's other writing too, the impulse to self-revelation goes hand in hand with the impulse to self-concealment—"every portrait that is painted with feeling," says the painter Basil Hallward in *The Picture of Dorian Gray,* "is a portrait of the artist."[45] Wilde was set on building into his play a series of veiled references to his own sexual orientation that, for modern readers and audiences at least, cumulatively subvert the play's superficially dominant concern with heterosexuality and marriage. Moreover, there are numerous biographical elements in *The Importance* that are less willful and deliberate on Wilde's part, or at least less carefully coded for concealment, and whose significance becomes clear only in the brighter retrospective light of our detailed knowledge of Wilde's public and private lives.

Even a casual reader of *The Importance* is struck by its cynical representation and critique of marriage. Just moments after the play begins, we are told that marriage is "the consequence of a misunderstanding" between young people and "not a very interesting subject." When, soon after, Jack ravenously devours Algernon's bread and butter (prefiguring Algernon's later devouring cucumber sandwiches and muffins), Algernon tells him that he is behaving as if he were "already married" to Gwendolen, the implication being that marriage forces the sublimation and transference of sexual desires, in this instance their transference to enormous appetite. The underlying notion here—that marriage between a man and a woman is sexless—is reinforced shortly afterward by Algernon's comment that "girls never marry the men they flirt with." "If you ever get married, . . . you will be very glad to know Bunbury," Algernon adds, explaining that "a man who marries without knowing Bunbury has a very tedious time of it" and that if Jack will not "know Bunbury," then his wife almost certainly will. In married life, "three is company and two is none," Algernon goes on to say, adding that the truth of his observation is borne out more readily in the modern English home than in "the corrupt French Drama." (Algernon's observation is all the more pointed if we know that Wilde himself was the author of a "corrupt French drama"—his play *Salomé,* written and first published in French and intended for London production with Sarah Bernhardt in the title role, was banned by the Censor before it could be publicly performed.) In the final moments of *The Importance,* when the newly betrothed couples "freeze" in a staged tableau, caught like statues in perpetual embrace, Wilde underscores the artifice and absurdity of this romantic and "earnest" resolution. Only the most sentimental in the audience can have forgotten that Algernon earlier observed that "divorces are made in Heaven,"[46] just as he had promised that if he ever got married, he would "try to forget the fact."

Modern English courtship rituals also come in for rough treatment in the play. In the hilarious scene in which Gwendolen tells Jack, "my ideal has always been to love some one of the name of Ernest"—and again in the scene in which Cecily tells Algernon that she fell in love with him before meeting him (when "dear Uncle Jack first confessed to us that he had a younger brother who was very wicked and bad") and that their engagement has already been undertaken and acted out within the pages of her own diary—Wilde implies that marriage has nothing to do with sex or even the physical presence of the betrothed. Shaped by socially sanctioned ideals, courtship rituals unfold according to a narrow, predictable script. Consider the famous scene in which Lady Bracknell interrogates Jack about his suitability to become her son-in-law. "An engagement should come upon a young girl as a surprise," Lady Bracknell tells Gwendolen, not because she is free to accept her betrothed at will but because only a mother— and a father, provided "his health permit him"—may decide when and to whom a girl might become engaged. Seemingly comic and absurd, the remark reminds us of the tremendous power exerted on the younger Wilde by his own mother, who has been seen as a real-life model for the fictive Lady Bracknell[47] and who had told Wilde eighteen months prior to his 1884 marriage to the eligible Constance Lloyd (and over a year before Wilde's engagement to her), "I would like her for a daughter-in-law."[48] An indomitable woman with strong convictions and a somewhat slavish devotion to etiquette, Lady Wilde played an active role in Wilde's courtship of his future wife,[49] since "when it came to her own sons she was more than prepared to consider how wealthy girls might provide automatic financial security for them."[50] "Bring home the bride," she only half jokingly instructed her devoted younger son in 1882: "1/4 of a million. Take a house in Park Lane."[51] But whereas Lady Wilde was reactive, Lady Bracknell is systematic. In the matter of selecting her daughter's betrothed, Lady Bracknell usually works from a list, she tells Jack—"the same list as the dear Duchess of Bolton; we work together in fact"—so she feels bound to tell Jack upfront, "you are not down on my list of eligible young men." Nonetheless, she is quite ready to enter his name, should Jack's answers prove to be what a really affectionate mother requires, and she proceeds to interrogate Jack about his occupation, age, education, income and investments, neighborhood of residence, political affiliation, and family background.

This scene is in part a send-up of prenuptial interviews that must have been dreaded by prospective husbands in the Victorian era, when men were generally older than their betrotheds and expected to have already established themselves in social and economic arenas. Lady Bracknell is "glad to hear" that Jack smokes because "a man should always have an occupation," and "there are far too many idle men in London as it is"; she is pleased to hear that Jack "knows nothing" because she "does not approve of anything that tampers with natural ignorance"; Jack's income of between seven and eight thousand a year from investments is "satisfactory" because "land has ceased to be either a profit or a pleasure"; and she expects Jack to own a town house as well as a country house because "a girl with a simple, unspoiled nature . . . could hardly be expected to reside in the country." His town house on the unfashionable side of Belgrave Square seems momentarily a stumbling block until a more intractable problem arises when Jack confesses he can claim no reputable lineage and is a foundling—left as an infant in a handbag deposited in the cloakroom at Victoria Station. "To be born, or at any rate bred, in a hand-bag," declares Lady Bracknell in one of the play's many immortal lines, "seems to me to display a contempt for the ordinary decencies of family life that reminds one of the worst excesses of the French Revolution." "You can hardly imagine," she tells Algernon with supreme hauteur, "that I and Lord Bracknell would dream of allowing our only daughter—a girl brought up with the utmost care—to marry into a cloak-room, and form an alliance with a parcel?"

Wilde's own marriage preparations suggest the scene is far more personal to Wilde than has generally been recognized. Lady Bracknell's preoccupations, for instance, mirror those of Lady Wilde, who expressed her joy at the prospect of Wilde's marriage in a letter of 28 February 1884: "we are greatly pleased at his marriage. A very nice pretty sensible girl—well-connected and well brought up—& a good fortune, about £1000 a year. They are looking for a house in London."[52] More importantly perhaps, Franny Moyle, in her recent biography of Wilde's wife, Constance, tells us that Constance's family was prepared to support the marriage "provided Oscar could prove himself sufficiently responsible."[53] Constance's grandfather and guardian, John Horatio Lloyd, was especially keen to question Wilde, Moyle tells us; however, like Lord Bracknell, he was too ill to interrogate Wilde directly himself, so it was left to Constance's Aunt Emily to discover from Wilde what his means were "of keeping a wife."[54] Only when Oscar could answer such points, Aunt Emily reminded Wilde, would the family give its consent. Moyle tells us that Wilde "must have made a good case for his capacity to earn an income" and was transparent about his debts (then around £1,500), so not only was the family's permission ultimately granted, but also a trust fund of £5,000 was specially created for the newlyweds "that would allow them to marry."[55] Algernon's observation, early in Act 1, that marriage proposals are a form of business proposition is perhaps less cynical and more personal than it seems, since Wilde himself, penniless, could never have married without the largesse of his wife's family.

Wilde's impoverishment on the point of marriage also finds its way into the scene. Like Lady Bracknell, Wilde knew from personal experience that "land has ceased either to be a profit or a pleasure." Upon the death of his father, Sir William Wilde, in 1876, Wilde inherited four small houses at Bray and a half share in a hunting lodge, at Illaunroe in Galway, while his mother inherited a stake in the house and small estate at Moytura that Sir William Wilde had built as a vacation home. But far from providing mother and son with income and security, the properties proved to be nothing but a headache. The Bray houses were heavily mortgaged, and in Lady Wilde's own words, "Nothing is to be had out of wretched Moytura,"[56] since rents from the few tenants on the estate were always delinquent. (As Gerald Hanberry remarks, "These were troubled times in Ireland. . . . The Land League agitation, which campaigned for tenants' rights, . . . and then Gladstone's reforming Land Acts meant that the Wildes would never receive much from Moytura.")[57] Wilde had trouble getting rent from his Bray tenants as well—in 1880, he called rents in Ireland "as extinct . . . as the dodo or moly,"[58] while the year before he had pleaded "the impossibility of getting rents" and "the extremely unsettled state of Ireland"[59] as excuses why he could not settle an unpaid bill. Within a few years of inheriting the Bray houses, he sold the leaseholds in them, though not without first entangling himself in a complex lawsuit in which he incurred heavy costs.[60] In short, Wilde, like his mother, was considerably impoverished by his father's death. As a result, as Gerald Hanberry puts it, "Oscar . . . believed that marriage was the only way out."[61]

The institution of marriage had been the focus of sharp debate ever since the writer Mona Caird had declared in the pages of the *Westminster Review* in 1888 "the present form of marriage" to be a "vexatious failure."[62] The play's critique participates in this wider ongoing public debate and extends the diatribe against marriage that is a constant theme in Wilde's writings going back to his essays "The American Man" and "The American Invasion," published in the *Court and Society Review* (originally subtitled *A Marriage Chronicle*) in 1887. But there is something decidedly cynical and personal about Wilde's treatment of marriage in *The Importance,* as even Wilde seems to acknowledge in the play ("it's perfectly easy to be cynical," Jack observes when Algernon comments how frequently the English home shows that "three is company and two none"). It is generally believed that Wilde did not have a homosexual affair until he had been married for two years, when he was seduced by Robert Ross in 1886. But by 1894, his marriage was a sham. It is hard to escape the conclusion that the play reflects Wilde's own unhappiness and sense of entrapment in marriage. There is, of course, Constance's point of view to consider as well. According to her latest biographer, Constance had in 1893 "finally admitted . . . that Oscar's friendship with Bosie was more than just that."[63] When *The Importance* opened on 14 February, she was away in Devon, and when she returned to London on 28 February, she had barely seen her husband in two months and returned home "to find 16 Tite Street empty and the servants still on board wages, as she had left them a month earlier."[64] (Constance returned on the very night that Oscar received Queensberry's fateful card. Her husband was staying at the Hotel Avondale, and it was from there that he wrote later that night, "My whole life seems ruined. . . . On the sand is my life spilt," resolving to commence his prosecution of the Marquess the very next day.)[65] Constance finally saw *The Importance* on 7 March, in the company of Wilde and Douglas, two nights before the commencement of the libel proceedings, and one can only imagine how she must have reacted, from her private box in the Dress Circle, while watching this "trivial" comedy unfold. According to Douglas, "she was very much agitated, and . . . she had tears in her eyes."[66]

In addition to the play's disenchanted critiques of marriage and courtship, there is one other important element in which the play reflects its author. The character Algernon Moncrieff resembles Wilde himself. It is clear, even before his appearance onstage, that like his creator, Algernon is a man of decidedly "aesthetic" tastes: the opening stage direction declares that the morning room in Algernon's flat in Half-Moon Street "is luxuriously and artistically furnished," and we first hear him playing the piano offstage, as we similarly first encounter Wilde's other "aesthetic" young men Dorian Gray (in *The Picture of Dorian Gray*) and Gilbert (in "The Critic as Artist"). The first-night program from the St. James's production underscores this Wilde-Algernon resemblance when it informs us that the set was furnished by the fashionable furniture dealer Frank Giles & Co., of Kensington High Street (purveyors of "Art Furniture," as the company's trade advertisements proclaim, and "Decorators and Complete House Furnishers"). Wilde may or may not have been involved in the selection of stage décor.[67] But the stage design/direction reminds us—as the first-night audience would have been aware—that before Wilde flourished as a playwright and man of letters, he had enjoyed a successful career on the lecture circuit speaking on "the House Beautiful," enjoining audiences in Britain and America to decorate their homes "by the procuring of articles which . . . are beautiful and fitted to impart pleasure."[68] Even before this, while still an undergraduate at Oxford, Wilde had become famous for filling his rooms with exquisite objects, not merely the blue china that he found it "harder and harder to live up to,"[69] according to one of his earliest and most famous quips, but also Tanagra statuettes, Greek rugs, and photographs of his favorite paintings.

In any case, it is clear the moment Algernon appears on stage that he is an aesthete: his mode of dress as much as his epigrammatic speech tells us so. Victorian photographs of Allan Aynsworth's performance as Algernon, in the first production, declare that Algernon is a character who takes immense pride in, and excessive care over, his personal appearance. On the opening night of *The Importance*, Wilde's friend Ada Leverson tells us, Wilde "was dressed with elaborate dandyism and a sort of florid sobriety. . . . [His] costume, which on another man might have appeared perilously like fancy-dress, and on his imitators was nothing less, seemed perfectly to suit him; he seemed at ease and to have a great look of the first gentleman in Europe."[70] In Act 2, Algernon accuses Jack of having "no taste in neckties," flaunting his own supremacy in this respect, and he has special suits and hats made solely for the days when he is "bunburying." In reply to Jack's charge that he is "always over-dressed," he will later confess, "if I am occasionally a little over-dressed, I make up for it by being always immensely over-educated." In December 1894, Wilde published a version of this epigram in "Phrases and Philosophies for the Use of the Young," in the *Chameleon*, where it had appeared over his own signature. Indeed the epigram is in effect *itself* a signature for the brilliant and always elegantly dressed Wilde. It is not just in Algernon's fastidious concern for his appearance that he resembles Wilde but also in his witty expression of that concern. Algernon, like his creator, is a dandy.

Earlier in the nineteenth century, Thomas Carlyle defined a dandy as "a Clothes-wearing Man, a man whose trade, office, and existence consists in the wearing of clothes."[71] But dandyism goes beyond an intense concern for sartorial elegance and is driven by the desire to create an aura of personal originality and beauty. "It is a kind of cult of the self," says the poet Charles Baudelaire, easily mistaken for egotism but in fact motivated by the desire to incarnate beauty in a world increasingly given over to industry, commerce, and the demands of material life.[72] As Wilde (drawing on Baudelaire) writes in *The Picture of Dorian Gray*, the dandy asserts through his clothing and personal adornments "the ab-solute modernity of beauty."[73] "His are all the delicate fopperies of Fashion," Wilde writes of another of his own invented

"Oscar Wilde, The Writer of The Play," sketch, by H. P. Seppings Wright, of Wilde on the opening night of *The Importance of Being Earnest*. *Illustrated London News*, February 23, 1895. Alderman Library, University of Virginia.

dandies (Lord Goring, in *An Ideal Husband*), and one sees immediately "that he stands in immediate relation to modern life—makes it indeed, and so masters it."[74] In both Wilde's and Algernon's cases, the dandy also asserts his androgyny, tempering traditionally masculine attributes with ones traditionally seen as feminine. The critic Camille Paglia has described all four of the play's young lovers as "androgynes of manners," inhabitants of a world narrowly circumscribed by the drawing room (personified on film by such actors as Cary Grant, David Niven, and Katharine Hepburn), each of whose sexuality is indeterminate and even sexless by conventional standpoints. The world of the androgyne of manners is effectively "an abstract circle," writes Paglia, "in which male and female, like mathematical ciphers, are equal and interchangeable" and "personality becomes a sexually undifferentiated mask."[75] Thus the male becomes "feminine in his careless, lounging passivity, the female masculine in her brilliant, aggressive wit," each seeming to possess "the profane sleekness of chic."[76] Paglia's observations explain why in our own day, *The Importance of Being Earnest* is so frequently performed in cross-dress, and they echo Wilde's own comment, made some six years before the composition of *The Importance,* that "of all the motives of dramatic curiosity used by our great playwrights, there is none more subtle or more fascinating than the ambiguity of the sexes."[77] The "difference of sex between the player and the part he represents," he continues, constitutes a "demand upon the imaginative capacities of the spectators," keeping them "from that over-realistic identification of the actor with his role which is one of the weak points of modern theatrical criticism."[78] But Paglia's (and Wilde's) comments apply more easily to Algernon than they do to Jack, who, until his existential crisis in Act 3, seems comfortably to inhabit the trappings of traditional masculine power, at least in public. He stands on his authority as a country gentleman, a justice of the peace, and the legal guardian of his niece Cecily (Russell Jackson observes that "as squire of Woolton, he takes his duties seriously and has undertaken the responsibilities of magistrate.")[79] Algernon, by contrast, represents a more fluid and unstable form of masculinity: unlike Jack, he has thoroughly internalized the "rules" of Bunburying, and for much of Act 1, he berates Jack for his attention to women and for his air of self-importance. Far more than Jack, Algernon is a man who "neglects his domestic duties," to employ Gwendolen's phrase, and who becomes at once "attractive" and "painfully effeminate" as a result.

Oscar Wilde himself embodied precisely those facets of character that Gwendolen finds attractive and effeminate. Contemporary accounts of Wilde frequently attest to his power to attract, repel, or confuse both men and women on account of a perceived effeminacy or ambiguity of gender. "The long locks of rich brown hair that waved across his forehead and undulated to his shoulders," writes Anna de Brémont, recalling her first meeting with him in 1882, "gave to his fine head an almost feminine beauty. It might have been the head of a splendid girl, were it not for the muscular white throat, fully displayed by the rolling collar and fantastic green silk necktie."[80] "There is a sort of horribly feminine air about him," remarked Julian Hawthorne (son of the novelist Nathaniel).[81] De Brémont even went so far as to posit that Wilde possessed a "feminine soul" and "was a slave to the capricious, critical feminine temperament, the feminine vanity and feminine weakness to temptation."[82] Alan Sinfield is surely right that the term *effeminacy,* like *masculinity* and *femininity,* is finally "an ideological construct, bearing no essential relation to the attributes of men and women."[83] But the point is that Wilde was perceived—particularly by those who were offended by him—as *effeminate, epicene,* and (in Edmond de Goncourt's phrase) *au sexe douteux*[84] (of ambiguous sex) and that increasingly such terms came to operate as code words for the sexual orientation we now term *homosexual.*[85]

However uncertain or ignorant Wilde's contemporaries might have been about the play's homosexual implications, the broad continuities between *The Importance of Being Earnest* and its author were not lost on them, especially in the years immediately after his downfall. "The affinity between the author and his work was unmistakeable," wrote the distinguished impresario and critic J. T. Grein (who himself mounted a controversial private production of Wilde's play *Salomé* in 1918).[86] Especially interesting is Grein's observation that the third act of *The Importance*—which some early reviewers "found . . . tedious" by comparison with the first two acts[87]—reflects the circumstances of its composition, when "the web was tightening round the man, and menaces of exposure must have rendered his gaiety forced."[88] The author "dominates his play," declared the critic for *Truth* on reviewing the first production in 1895.[89] *The Importance* is Wilde's most "sincere" and "serious" play, declared the critic and playwright St. John Hankin upon reviewing the first collected edition of Wilde's plays in 1908.[90] "One might easily conceive an artist capable of producing so clean-cut and crystalline a comedy as *The Importance of Being Earnest* . . . disappearing quite out of sight, in the manner so commended by Flaubert. . . . But so far from disappearing, Oscar Wilde manages to emphasize himself and his imposing presence only the more startlingly and flagrantly," remarks John Cowper Powys.[91] The greatness of *The Importance of Being Earnest* comes not from the play's separateness from Wilde's life and personality, from its perceived autonomy as a work of "art" existing merely for the sake of art, but from its inseparability from these things. "It is a terrible thing for a man to find out that . . . he has been speaking nothing but the truth," declares Jack, newly christened as Ernest, at the end of the play. From a twenty-first-century perspective, it is possible to see that in *The Importance of Being Earnest,* Wilde may have been speaking more truthfully than even he realized.

Notes

1. Ada Leverson, *Letters to the Sphinx from Oscar Wilde, with Reminiscences of the Author* (London: Duckworth, 1930), 26.

2. As Leverson later recalled, "everyone was repeating his 'mots.' . . . 'To meet Mr. Oscar Wilde' was put on the most exclusive of invitation cards" (ibid., 29).

3. Ibid., 27.

4. William Archer, signed review of *The Importance of Being Earnest, World*, 20 Feb. 1895, repr. in *Oscar Wilde: The Critical Heritage*, ed. Karl Beckson (London: Routledge and Kegan Paul, 1970), 190.

5. "H. F." [Hamilton Fyfe], notice of *The Importance of Being Earnest, New York Times*, 17 Feb. 1895, repr. in Beckson, *Oscar Wilde*, 188–89.

6. The first New York production, which opened at the Empire Theater on 22 April 1895, closed after just one week.

7. Printed programs for the first production survive in both the original and the later redacted version (i.e., both with and without Wilde's name appearing). When Irene Vanburgh, the actress who performed Gwendolen in the first production, writes that Wilde's name "was obliterated on all the playbills," she means that Alexander went to the trouble of having new posters—the large broadsheets pasted to the theater's façade and front columns—as well as new programs printed without attribution of the playwright. No poster for the opening run of *The Importance* is known to survive, but Wilde's first biographer,

Robert Sherard, tells us that Wilde's name was "effaced both on posters and programmes" (Sherard, *The Life of Oscar Wilde* [London: T. Werner Laurie, 1906], 362).

8. Anonymous pencil annotation to St. James's Theatre program, quoted in *Oscar Wilde's "The Importance of Being Earnest": A Reconstructive Critical Edition of the Text of the First Production,* ed. and annotated by Joseph Donohue, with Ruth Berggren (Gerrards Cross, UK: Colin Smythe, 1995), 69. Wilde's agent, Elizabeth Marbury, attributes the play's closing to its actor-producer George Alexander, who "lacked the courage to continue," "was afraid of public opinion," and "dared not be classed with the few friends who stood loyally by Wilde even in his darkest moments" (Marbury, "The Last Days of Oscar Wilde" [1923], repr. in *Oscar Wilde: Interviews and Recollections,* ed. E. H. Mikhail, 2 vols. [London: Macmillan, 1979], 2:436).

9. Quoted in Brian Reade, *Sexual Heretics: Male Homosexuality in English Literature from 1850 to 1900* (New York: Coward-McCann, 1970), 52n1.

10. Sidney Grundy, letter to the editor, *Daily Telegraph,* 8 Apr. 1898, 5.

11. "It made some of us angry," wrote the distinguished critic and producer J. T. Grein, when Alexander revived Wilde's play in 1901 under the byline "by the author of *Lady Windermere's Fan*" (signed review of 1901 production, *Sunday Times,* 8 Dec. 1901, repr. in Beckson, *Oscar Wilde,* 239). "Though it was good to use the artist's work," Grein understood Alexander to be saying, "his name was not sufficiently honorable to be given out." It was not until the long and profitable 1909 revival that Alexander deemed it safe to reattach Wilde's name to the play.

12. Oscar Wilde to Reginald Turner, postmarked 20 Mar. 1899, *Complete Letters of Oscar Wilde*, ed. Merlin Holland and Rupert Hart-Davis (New York: Henry Holt, 2000), 1132 (hereafter cited as *CL*).

13. Although Shaw reviewed the play in the *Saturday Review* on 23 Feb. 1895 (repr. in Beckson, *Oscar Wilde*, 194–95), these phrases are taken from his memoir "My Memories of Oscar Wilde," printed as an appendix in Frank Harris, *Oscar Wilde* (1916; repr., New York: Dorset, 1989), 333.

14. Archer, review of *The Importance of Being Earnest*, 189.

15. Unsigned review of *The Importance of Being Earnest*, *Truth*, 21 Feb. 1895, repr. in Beckson, *Oscar Wilde*, 191.

16. "Appendix B: The 1891 Preface to *The Picture of Dorian Gray*," in Oscar Wilde, *The Picture of Dorian Gray: An Annotated Uncensored Edition*, ed. Nicholas Frankel (Cambridge, MA: Harvard University Press, 2011), 273.

17. Ibid.

18. Marquess of Queensberry, letter to Lord Alfred Douglas, 3 Apr. 1894, quoted in Merlin Holland, *The Real Trial of Oscar Wilde* (New York: Perennial, 2004), 215.

19. Holland, *Real Trial of Oscar Wilde*, 80 (hereafter cited parenthetically in the text by page number).

20. In 1890, Wilde had refuted the notion that *Dorian Gray* was a "poisonous book, . . . heavy with the mephitic odours of moral and spiritual putrefaction" (unsigned rev. of *The Picture of Dorian Gray*, *Daily Chronicle*, 30 June 1890, repr. in Beckson, *Oscar Wilde*, 72) by writing, "I am quite incapable of understanding how any work of art

can be criticized from a moral standpoint" (Wilde to the editor of the *St. James's Gazette*, 25 June 1890, *CL* 428) and "each man sees his own sin in Dorian Gray. What Dorian Gray's sins are no one knows. He who finds them has brought them" (Wilde to the editor of the *Scots Observer*, 9 July 1890, *CL* 439).

21. In late February 1895, Wilde was served with three writs for debts totaling about £400, "principally for cigarettes and cigarette cases," and on 24 April 1895, two days before his first criminal trial, the contents of Wilde's Tite Street home were sold by bailiffs seeking to recover these debts (*Morning*, 25 Apr. 1895, repr. in Jonathan Goodman, *The Oscar Wilde File* [London: Allison & Busby, 1988], 100). Later in the year, Wilde (now incarcerated in Wandsworth Prison) was served with a receiving order—resulting ultimately in his bankruptcy—on account of unpaid debts of £3,591, including £233 for "tobacco, wine, jewelry, flowers, etc.," as well as the £95 owed to the Savoy and Willis (*Times*, 13 Nov. 1895, repr. in Goodman, *Oscar Wilde File*, 138). Although the receiving order was initiated by the Marquess of Queensberry, attempting to recover £677 in costs awarded him by the courts as a result of Wilde's failed libel suit, Wilde had lived on the brink of financial disaster since long before his action against Queensberry: as Wilde himself put matters before the commencement of the libel suit and roughly one month before his arrest, "my life is so marred and maimed by extravagance" (Wilde to George Alexander, Feb. 1895, *CL* 633). Indeed, only the success of *The Importance of Being Earnest* in its opening weeks—in particular, an advance of £1,000 against future royalties, made to Wilde by the actor-manager George Alexander—had staved off the mountain of debt. Alexander's advance, which was in two installments dated 28 February and 6 March, came at a hefty price—50 percent of all future

earnings from productions of the play in North America—although Wilde's arrest and the subsequent closing of the play meant that this price would never be paid in full. See "Memorandum of Supplementary Agreement," dated 6 March 1895, in "Papers Relating to Oscar Wilde's Literary Estate," File 6, Box 1, Bodleian Library, Oxford University.

22. Antony Edmonds, "'You Will Come, Won't You': Bosie's Visits to Worthing in 1894," *Wildean* 39 (July 2011): 40. Edmonds is thinking mainly of Douglas's attempt to persuade Wilde to allow him to stay in the house with a questionable companion, but other "illicit pleasures" included regular sailing trips, in the company of Wilde and two young, male local acquaintances (with one of whom, Alphonse Conway, Wilde was sexually involved), and a four-day excursion with Wilde to Dieppe, on the other side of the English Channel.

23. The three-day trip to Brighton is memorably described in *De Profundis,* though Wilde's account there, written in jail over two years after the events described, cannot be relied on, colored as it is by his belated efforts to repudiate Douglas's influence on his life (Wilde errs, for instance, in identifying the Metropole Hotel as the Grand Hotel). As Merlin Holland has observed, the jaunt to Brighton was still unpaid for at the time of Wilde's arrest (*Real Trial of Oscar Wilde,* 310n118).

24. Russell Jackson, "The Importance of Being Earnest," in *The Cambridge Companion to Oscar Wilde,* ed. Peter Raby (Cambridge: Cambridge University Press, 1997), 168.

25. An edition of the play in four acts was published in German as early as 1903 in Leipzig, Germany, although English-language readers

remained unaware of it for at least another forty years. In 1956, the New York Public Library published *The Importance of Being Earnest* . . . *in Four Acts as Originally Written by Oscar Wilde,* edited by Sarah Augusta Dickson, based on manuscript drafts in the New York Public Library and the British Library. In 1957, Methuen published a different four-act version of Wilde's play, edited by Wilde's son Vyvyan Holland, based partly on the 1903 German translation but also including "witty lines from different stages of the history of the play" (introduction to *The Definitive Four-Act Version of "The Importance of Being Earnest,"* ed. Ruth Berggren [New York: Vanguard, 1987], 35). This hybrid version from 1957 was subsequently incorporated into Collins's *The Complete Works of Oscar Wilde,* edited by Vyvyan Holland in 1966 (London: Collins) and still in print today under the editorship of Merlin Holland.

26. This is true of the three-act text published and seen through the press by Wilde in 1899 as well as the text of the first production of 1895, also in three acts, brilliantly reconstructed by its editor, Joseph Donohue, in 1995 (*Oscar Wilde's "The Importance of Being Earnest"*; see note 8). As Donohue shows, the first production text was quite distinct from the one Wilde later saw through the press, though it was in fact quite fluid and differed slightly at the end of the play's run from the first-night version, reflecting "a point in the production when the business has been fixed and is familiar to the actors and stage manager" (83).

27. See Christopher Craft, "Alias Bunbury," *Representations* 31 (Summer 1990): 19–46; Craven Mackie, "Bunbury Pure and Simple," *Modern Drama* 41, no. 2 (1998): 327–30; and Donohue, *Oscar Wilde's "The Importance of Being Earnest,"* 124. As Kerry Powell has argued ("Algernon's Other Brothers," in his *Oscar Wilde and the Theatre of*

the 1890s [Cambridge: Cambridge University Press, 1990], 124–27),
the concept of bunburying—as well as the name Bunbury—could
have been suggested to Wilde by the success of *Godpapa,* a popular
farce by F. C. Philips and Charles Brookfield, staged at the Court
Theatre in 1891–1892, in which young "Reggie" describes the
imaginary ailment of an acquaintance named Bunbury in order to
indulge his own whims without interference.

28. Joel Fineman, "The Significance of Literature: *The Importance of
Being Earnest,*" *October* 15 (1980), repr. in *Critical Essays on Oscar
Wilde,* ed. Regenia Gagnier (New York: G. K. Hall, 1991), 113.

29. Alan Sinfield, " 'Effeminacy' and 'Femininity': Sexual Politics in
Wilde's Comedies," *Modern Drama* 37, no. 1 (Spring 1994): 35.
Likewise, Sinfield observes that there are no historical grounds for
Joel Fineman's unsupported assertion that "Bunbury . . . [was]
British slang for a male brothel" (35).

30. This theory was first propounded by Aleister Crowley in 1913
and is discussed by Timothy D'Arch Smith in his *Bunbury: Two
Notes* (Bicary, France: Winged Lion, 1998).

31. Wilde, letter to William Rothenstein, Aug. 1894, *CL* 601 ("amuse
himself"); see also Wilde, letter to Lord Alfred Douglas, 13 Aug.
1894, *CL* 601–2. For details of Wilde's affair with Conway, who was
later to act as a witness against Wilde in the failed libel case that
led to Wilde's prosecution, see Neil McKenna, *The Secret Life of
Oscar Wilde* (New York: Basic Books, 2005), 297–99; and Antony
Edmonds, "Alphonse Conway—the 'Bright Happy Boy' of 1894,"
Wildean 38 (Jan. 2011): 18–43. Edmonds writes that Wilde's
relations with Conway were not solely or even principally sexual:
"affection, good fellowship, and enjoyment of time spent in

innocent pursuits" such as sailing and bathing "were an important component of his association with Alphonse" ("Alphonse Conway," 38).

32. Peter Raby, "Wilde, and How to Be Modern," in *Wilde Writings, Contextual Conditions,* ed. Joseph Bristow (Toronto: University of Toronto Press, 2003), 152.

33. Oscar Wilde, *The Importance of Being Earnest,* ed. Samuel Lyndon Gladden (Peterborough, ON: Broadview, 2010), 77n1.

34. Max Nordau, *Degeneration* (1892; English trans., New York: D. Appleton, 1895), 196, 519.

35. J. G. F. Nicholson, *Love in Earnest: Sonnets, Ballades, and Lyrics* (London: Elliot Stock, 1892), 61. Although Wilde's reactions to Nicholson's *Love in Earnest* are unrecorded, another of Nicholson's works, his prose poem "The Shadow of the End," appeared alongside Wilde's "Phrases and Philosophies for the Use of the Young" in the December 1894 number of the Oxford undergraduate magazine the *Chameleon,* edited by the homosexual writer John Francis Bloxam. Bloxam, whom Wilde met late in 1894 and called "an undergraduate of strange beauty" (Wilde, letter to Ada Leverson, early Dec. 1894, *CL* 625)—and who himself authored a homosexual tale titled "The Priest and the Acolyte" that had also appeared in the *Chameleon*— may have inspired the name of Jack's tenant Lady Bloxham, "a lady considerably advanced in years," whose age Lady Bracknell finds to be "no guarantee of respectability of character."

36. See Timothy D'Arch Smith, *Love in Earnest* (London: Routledge, 1970); and Karl Beckson, *London in the 1890s* (New York: Norton, 1992), chap. 8.

37. Herbert Fry, *London: Illustrated by Twenty Bird's-Eye Views* (1895), quoted in Donohue, *Oscar Wilde's "The Importance of Being Earnest,"* 120.

38. Donohue, *Oscar Wilde's "The Importance of Being Earnest,"* 121–22.

39. Quoted in ibid., 121.

40. Regenia Gagnier, *Idylls of the Marketplace: Oscar Wilde and the Victorian Public* (Stanford, CA: Stanford University Press, 1986), 46.

41. Wilde to Lord Alfred Douglas, circa 17 Feb. 1895, *CL* 632.

42. Wilde to Lord Alfred Douglas, 2 Jun. 1897, *CL* 874.

43. See Nicholas Frankel, textual introduction to *The Picture of Dorian Gray: An Annotated Uncensored Edition,* 43–44.

44. "Mr. Oscar Wilde on Mr. Oscar Wilde," *St. James Gazette,* 18 Jan. 1895, repr. in Mikhail, *Oscar Wilde,* 1:250.

45. *The Picture of Dorian Gray: An Annotated Uncensored Edition,* 77.

46. A play on the proverb that marriages are made in heaven, Algernon's remark "Divorces are made in Heaven" obliges us to reflect how near to divorce Wilde himself came in 1897, when he was still in prison and his wife, Constance, was considering suing him for divorce. In the event, Constance (who never saw Wilde again) settled for a permanent, legal separation from Wilde—almost certainly to spare her children and Wilde himself, since to obtain a divorce, she would have had to prove that Wilde had committed sodomy, thus inflicting a further, even more severe, prison sentence on him.

47. In discussing Lady Wilde's influence on the character of Lady Bracknell, Patrick Horan says that "Lady Bracknell . . . resembles

that socially conscious side of Speranza [Lady Wilde's penname],"
that she "gives voice to Speranza's belief that one should act in
accordance with the rules of society," and that "Wilde exaggerates
Lady Bracknell's desire to create an ideal marriage for her daughter,
in part, to undermine Speranza's notion that marriages should be
ideal" (Horan, *The Importance of Being Paradoxical: Maternal
Presence in the Works of Oscar Wilde* [Madison, NJ: Fairleigh Dick-
inson University Press, 1997], 107–8).

48. Lady Jane Wilde to Oscar Wilde, Oct. 1882, in *Lady Jane
Wilde's Letters to Oscar Wilde 1875–1895,* ed. Karen S. Tipper
(Lewiston, NY: Edwin Mellen, 2011), 91.

49. As Franny Moyle observes, soon after Lady Wilde's move to
London in 1879, securing "a good match" for her two sons became
"a priority" (Moyle, *Constance: The Tragic and Scandalous Life of
Mrs. Oscar Wilde* [London: John Murray, 2011], 45). Joy Melville
tells us that Lady Wilde, "with Oscar's bachelor state in mind,
invited Constance to her salons" (Melville, *Mother of Oscar: The
Life of Jane Francesca Wilde* [London: John Murray, 1994], 161)
and, during Wilde's yearlong absence lecturing in North America,
"made a point of keeping in touch with Constance" (176). See also
Lady Wilde's letter to Constance of May 1883, in which she expresses
how "desolated" Oscar and she were at "not seeing you yesterday"
(in *Lady Jane Wilde's Letters to Constance Wilde, Friends and
Acquaintances,* ed. Karen S. A. Tipper [Lewiston, NY: Edwin
Mellen, 2013], 19).

50. Moyle, *Constance,* 63.

51. Lady Jane Wilde to Oscar Wilde, 23 Jan. 1882, in Tipper, *Lady
Jane Wilde's Letters to Oscar Wilde,* 65.

52. Lady Jane Wilde to Mrs. Philippa Knott, 28 Feb. 1884, in Tipper, *Lady Jane Wilde's Letters to Constance Wilde,* 110. Lady Wilde's expression of joy at the prospect of Wilde's marriage may be tempered by the fact that the recipient of this letter was the sister of Florence Balcombe, whom Wilde had once loved and possibly intended marrying but who had in 1878 married Bram Stoker instead (see Wilde's three letters to Florence Balcombe, written shortly after hearing of her betrothal to Stoker, in late September and early October 1878, *CL* 71–73). Indeed Lady Wilde's expression of joy at the prospect of Wilde's marriage is immediately prefaced by the comment that while "Bram is always very attentive & kind," Florence is rarely seen and "never comes here" (Jane Wilde to Knott, 28 Feb. 1884, 110).

53. Moyle, *Constance,* 76.

54. Ibid.

55. Ibid., 77.

56. Quoted in Gerald Hanberry, *More Lives than One: The Remarkable Wilde Family through the Generations* (Cork, Ireland: Collins, 2011), 191.

57. Ibid., 191.

58. Wilde to Oscar Browning, mid-February 1880, *CL* 87.

59. Wilde to an unidentified correspondent, received 5 Nov. 1879, *CL* 84.

60. See Wilde's letters to William Ward, tentatively dated by the editors of Wilde's correspondence 11 July 1878 and c. 24 July 1878, *CL* 69–70.

61. Hanberry, *More Lives than One*, 192.

62. Mona Caird, "Marriage" (1888), repr. in her *The Morality of Marriage and Other Essays* (London: George Redway, 1897), 105.

63. Moyle, *Constance*, 229.

64. Ibid., 11.

65. Wilde to Robert Ross, 28 Feb. 1895, *CL* 634.

66. Alfred Douglas, *The Autobiography of Lord Alfred Douglas* (London: Martin Secker, 1929), 59.

67. Early reviewers imply that Wilde was involved in questions of set design when they praise the "carnation-green" décor of Jack's morning room in Act 3. See note 1 in Act 3, below.

68. Kevin H. F. O'Brien, " 'The House Beautiful': A Reconstruction of Oscar Wilde's American Lecture," *Victorian Studies* 17, no. 4 (June 1974): 401.

69. For discussion of Wilde's quip "I find it harder and harder every day to live up to my blue china," see Richard Ellmann, *Oscar Wilde* (New York: Knopf, 1988), 45.

70. Leverson, *Letters to the Sphinx*, 33–34.

71. Thomas Carlyle, *Sartor Resartus* (1833–1834), repr. in *A Carlyle Reader*, ed. G. B. Tennyson (Cambridge: Cambridge University Press, 1984), 313. As Algernon's comment to Jack "I never saw anybody take so long to dress" implies, Jack is a dandy too, albeit one less reconciled to the fact. Along with Algernon's "strikingly modern" shirt cuffs, one early reviewer praised the "effusive loveliness" of Jack's neckties (unsigned review of *The Importance of Being Earnest, Truth*, 193).

72. Charles Baudelaire, "The Painter of Modern Life," in *The Painter of Modern Life and Other Essays,* trans. and ed. Jonathan Mayne (London: Phaidon, 1995), 27.

73. *The Picture of Dorian Gray: An Annotated Uncensored Edition,* 190.

74. Stage direction, opening of Act 3, *An Ideal Husband,* in *Complete Works of Oscar Wilde,* ed. Merlin Holland, rev. ed. (London: Harper Collins, 1994), 553.

75. Camille Paglia, *Sexual Personae* (New Haven, CT: Yale University Press, 1990), 531–32.

76. Ibid., 532.

77. "The Portrait of Mr. W. H.," in *Complete Works of Oscar Wilde,* ed. Merlin Holland, 330.

78. Ibid.

79. Russell Jackson, editorial note to "The Persons of the Play," in Wilde, *The Importance of Being Earnest,* ed. Russell Jackson (1980; repr. London: A. C. Black/New York: W. W. Norton, 1988), 4.

80. Anna de Brémont, *Oscar Wilde and His Mother: A Memoir* (London: Everett, 1911), 25.

81. Quoted in Ellmann, *Oscar Wilde,* 59.

82. De Brémont, *Oscar Wilde and His Mother,* 15–16.

83. Alan Sinfield, *The Wilde Century: Effeminacy, Oscar Wilde, and the Queer Moment* (New York: Columbia University Press, 1994), 26.

84. Edmond de Goncourt, quoted in Ellmann, *Oscar Wilde,* 230.

85. For a counterargument, see Sinfield, "'Effeminacy' and 'Femininity.'"

86. J. T. Grein, signed article on Wilde as a dramatist, *Sunday Special*, 9 and 16 Dec. 1900, repr. in Beckson, *Oscar Wilde,* 233.

87. Archer, signed review of *The Importance of Being Earnest,* 191.

88. Grein, signed review of *The Importance of Being Earnest,* 239.

89. Unsigned review of *The Importance of Being Earnest, Truth,* 193.

90. St. John Hankin, "The Collected Plays of Oscar Wilde" (1908), repr. in Beckson, *Oscar Wilde,* 284.

91. John Cowper Powys, "Oscar Wilde" (1916), repr. as "John Cowper Powys on Wilde as a Symbolic Figure" in Beckson, *Oscar Wilde,* 358.

* *The Importance of Being Earnest* was subtitled "A Serious Comedy
for Trivial People" until shortly before its opening night. On reviewing
it, George Bernard Shaw damned Wilde's play with faint praise as
"a farcical comedy," and even Wilde himself once professed it "too
farcical . . . [to] be made part of a repertoire of serious or classical
pieces" (Wilde to George Alexander, September [?] 1894, *Complete
Letters of Oscar Wilde*, ed. Merlin Holland and Rupert Hart-Davis [New
York: Henry Holt, 2000], 610 [hereafter cited as *CL*]). Wilde's debts to
such popular farces as W. S. Gilbert's *Engaged* (1877) and W. Lestocq
and E. M. Robson's *The Foundling* (1894) have frequently been noted
by critics. But in writing his "trivial comedy," Wilde also had in mind
such "serious" mainstays of the late-Victorian theater as the social
dramas of Arthur Wing Pinero and Henry Arthur Jones, the latter
of whom had once written that Victorians must "put aside farcical
comedy, burlesque, and comic opera" and stage only "plays of serious
intention, . . . plays that implicitly assert the value and dignity of human
life, . . . full of meaning and importance" (Jones, "The Dramatic Outlook"
[1884], repr. in Jones, *The Renascence of the English Drama* [London:
Macmillan, 1895], 170–71).

THE IMPORTANCE OF
BEING EARNEST

A TRIVIAL COMEDY FOR
SERIOUS PEOPLE*

1. Justice of the Peace (i.e., magistrate), signifying that Jack is a man of means and takes seriously his responsibilities as a country gentleman. Worthing—"a seaside resort," as Jack explains to Lady Bracknell in Act 1—was where Wilde retired to write *The Importance of Being Earnest* and also to enjoy a summer holiday with his family, in the summer of 1894, only to have his plans turned upside down by three separate visits from Lord Alfred Douglas as well as by a brief, sexually charged affair with a sixteen-year-old resident of Worthing named Alphonse Conway.

2. Deriving from Norman French, and originally meaning "with a moustache" (from Old French *grenon, gernon* 'moustache'), the name *Algernon* was heavily favored from the fifteenth century onward by male descendants of William de Percy, a companion of William the Conqueror (*A Dictionary of Names,* ed. Patrick Hanks et al., 2nd ed. [Oxford: Oxford University Press, 2006]). "It is rather an aristocratic name," Algernon later says of his own name: "half the chaps who get into Bankruptcy Court are called Algernon." In early drafts of the play, Algernon was "Lord Alfred," and he was the son, not the nephew, of the imperious Lady Bracknell (originally "Lady Brancaster").

3. Doctor of Divinity. A *chasuble* is the outermost garment worn by priests in celebrating the Eucharist. As Russell Jackson observes, Chasuble's name, as well as his obsession with the Primitive Church, suggests that he is a priest with "High Church" leanings (editorial note to "The Persons of the Play," in Wilde, *The Importance of Being Earnest,* ed. Russell Jackson [1980; repr. London: A. C. Black/New York: W. W. Norton, 1988], 4).

4. Wilde's publisher at the time he composed *The Importance* was named Lane, though Wilde was contemptuous of his intellect and was beginning to fall out with him.

THE PERSONS OF THE PLAY

John Worthing, J.P.[1]
Algernon Moncrieff[2]
Rev. Canon Chasuble, D.D.[3]
Merriman, Butler
Lane, Manservant[4]
Lady Bracknell[5]
Hon. Gwendolen Fairfax
Cecily Cardew
Miss Prism, Governess[6]

THE SCENES OF THE PLAY

ACT I. Algernon Moncrieff's Flat in Half-Moon Street, W.[7]

ACT II. The Garden at the Manor House, Woolton.

ACT III. Drawing-Room at the Manor House, Woolton.[8]

TIME: The Present.[9]

5. Bracknell, a town in Berkshire, was where Lady Queensberry, Lord Alfred Douglas's mother, resided after her 1887 divorce from the Marquess of Queensberry.

6. Like Lady Bracknell, Miss Prism is partly inspired by Miss Penelope Prude in Dion Boucicault's 1842 farce *A Lover by Proxy*.

7. Half-Moon Street was one of the most fashionable streets in London's wealthy Mayfair district, less than a mile from the theater where *The Importance of Being Earnest* was first performed. "W" is the Victorian postal code for the area immediately west of London's center. The first-night playbill locates Algernon's flat in Piccadilly, a decidedly more risqué location, not in Half-Moon Street.

8. The first-night playbill, as well as the stage direction at the head of Act 3, locates Act 3 in the morning room at the Manor House, Woolton. "Drawing-Room," a holdover from early drafts of the play, is an error, unnoticed and uncorrected by Wilde as he revised the text for publication.

9. "Whether a comedy should deal with modern life," Wilde writes, "whether its subject should be society or middle-class existence, these are questions purely [for] the artist's own choice. Personally I like comedy to be intensely modern" (Wilde, to an unidentified correspondent, [1894?], *CL*, 626).

———

1. For the first London production, the furnishings in Algernon's flat were specially bought from the fashionable furniture dealer Frank Giles of Kensington. "My plays are difficult plays to produce well," said Wilde: "they require artistic setting on the stage, a good company that knows something of the style essential to high comedy, beautiful dresses, [and] a sense of the luxury of modern life" (Wilde to Grace

ACT ONE

SCENE: Morning-room in Algernon's flat in Half-Moon Street. The room is luxuriously and artistically furnished.[1] *The sound of a piano is heard in the adjoining room. Lane is arranging afternoon tea on the table, and after the music has ceased, Algernon enters.*

Algernon. Did you hear what I was playing, Lane?

Lane. I didn't think it polite to listen, sir.

Algernon. I'm sorry for that, for your sake. I don't play accurately—any one can play accurately—but I play with wonderful expression. As far as the piano is concerned, sentiment is my forte. I keep science for Life.

Lane. Yes, sir.

Algernon. And, speaking of the science of Life, have you got the cucumber sandwiches cut for Lady Bracknell?

Lane. Yes, sir. [*Hands them on a salver.*]

Algernon. [*Inspects them, takes two, and sits down on the sofa.*] Oh! . . . by the way, Lane, I see from your book that on Thursday night, when Lord Shoreham and

Hawthorne, 4 Oct. 1894, in *Complete Letters of Oscar Wilde*, ed.
Merlin Holland and Rupert Hart-Davis [New York: Henry Holt, 2000],
617 [hereafter cited as *CL*]).

2. Lane, who later declares, "I do my best to give satisfaction," is a
model of imperturbability. In this respect, he resembles Phipps,
Lord Goring's butler in Wilde's play *An Ideal Husband*, whose
"distinction ... is his impassivity," Wilde tells us in the stage directions
to that play, and who represents "the dominance of form" (stage
direction, opening of Act 3, *An Ideal Husband*, in *Complete Works
of Oscar Wilde*, ed. Merlin Holland, rev. ed. [London: Harper Collins,
1994], 553).

Mr. Worthing were dining with me, eight bottles of champagne are entered as having been consumed.

Lane. Yes, sir; eight bottles and a pint.

Algernon. Why is it that at a bachelor's establishment the servants invariably drink the champagne? I ask merely for information.

Lane. I attribute it to the superior quality of the wine, sir. I have often observed that in married households the champagne is rarely of a first-rate brand.[2]

Algernon. Good heavens! Is marriage so demoralizing as that?

Lane. I believe it *is* a very pleasant state, sir. I have had very little experience of it myself up to the present. I have only been married once. That was in consequence of a misunderstanding between myself and a young person.

Algernon. [*Languidly.*] I don't know that I am much interested in your family life, Lane.

Lane. No, sir; it is not a very interesting subject. I never think of it myself.

Algernon. Very natural, I am sure. That will do, Lane, thank you.

Lane. Thank you, sir. [*Lane goes out.*]

Algernon. Lane's views on marriage seem somewhat lax. Really, if the lower orders don't set us a good example, what

3. This is the first of two "asides" in which Algernon, left alone on stage briefly, addresses the audience directly: his use of "us" ("don't set us a good example") establishes complicity with the audience.

4. The first of many mentions of pleasure. In "Phrases and Philosophies for the Use of the Young" (*Chameleon*, December 1894), Wilde had written, "Pleasure is the only thing one should live for. Nothing ages like happiness."

5. As Algernon is perfectly aware, Shropshire, in the West Midlands, bordering Wales, is one of the most rural and sparsely populated counties in England.

on earth is the use of them? They seem, as a class, to have absolutely no sense of moral responsibility.[3]

[*Enter Lane.*]

Lane. Mr. Ernest Worthing.

[*Enter Jack. Lane goes out.*]

Algernon. How are you, my dear Ernest? What brings you up to town?

Jack. Oh, pleasure, pleasure! What else should bring one anywhere?[4] Eating as usual, I see, Algy!

Algernon. [*Stiffly.*] I believe it is customary in good society to take some slight refreshment at five o'clock. Where have you been since last Thursday?

Jack. [*Sitting down on the sofa.*] In the country.

Algernon. What on earth do you do there?

Jack. [*Pulling off his gloves.*] When one is in town one amuses oneself. When one is in the country one amuses other people. It is excessively boring.

Algernon. And who are the people you amuse?

Jack. [*Airily.*] Oh, neighbours, neighbours.

Algernon. Got nice neighbours in your part of Shropshire?[5]

Jack. Perfectly horrid! Never speak to one of them.

6. "Why such reckless extravagance in one so young?" was added in 1899. As Joseph Donohue observes (editorial note, *Oscar Wilde's "The Importance of Being Earnest": A Reconstructive Critical Edition of the Text of the First Production,* ed. and annotated by Joseph Donohue, with Ruth Berggren [Gerrards Cross, UK: Colin Smythe, 1995], 110), the line echoes (and inverts) a remark that Wilde made to Alfred Douglas in his 1897 prison letter *De Profundis:* "Your reckless extravagance was not a crime. Youth is always extravagant" (Wilde to Lord Alfred Douglas, Jan.–Mar. 1897, *CL* 770).

7. In order to marry his future wife, Constance Lloyd, Wilde (who had no means of supporting a wife) was heavily reliant on the largesse of Constance's grandfather John Horatio Lloyd. The marriage was eventually enabled through Lloyd's creation of a trust fund for the couple, though first Wilde was obliged to show that his debts were not excessive and that he was capable of earning a reasonable income.

Algernon. How immensely you must amuse them! [*Goes over and takes sandwich.*] By the way, Shropshire is your county, is it not?

Jack. Eh? Shropshire? Yes, of course. Hallo! Why all these cups? Why cucumber sandwiches? Why such reckless extravagance in one so young?[6] Who is coming to tea?

Algernon. Oh! merely Aunt Augusta and Gwendolen.

Jack. How perfectly delightful!

Algernon. Yes, that is all very well; but I am afraid Aunt Augusta won't quite approve of your being here.

Jack. May I ask why?

Algernon. My dear fellow, the way you flirt with Gwendolen is perfectly disgraceful. It is almost as bad as the way Gwendolen flirts with you.

Jack. I am in love with Gwendolen. I have come up to town expressly to propose to her.

Algernon. I thought you had come up for pleasure? . . . I call that business.[7]

Jack. How utterly unromantic you are!

Algernon. I really don't see anything romantic in proposing. It is very romantic to be in love. But there is nothing romantic about a definite proposal. Why, one may be accepted. One usually is, I believe. Then the excitement is all

8. In April 1897, Wilde lamented that his friendship with Alfred Douglas, having already brought him to the Criminal Court and the Bankruptcy Court, had now brought him to the dock of the Divorce Court. Nonetheless, he was briefly reconciled to the inevitability of a divorce: "Whether I am married or not is a matter that does not concern me. For years I disregarded the tie" (Wilde to Robert Ross, 1 Apr. 1897, CL, 785). In the event, Constance settled for a separation agreement, sparing her husband, children, and herself potentially devastating divorce proceedings.

over. The very essence of romance is uncertainty. If ever I get married, I'll certainly try to forget the fact.

Jack. I have no doubt about that, dear Algy. The Divorce Court was specially invented for people whose memories are so curiously constituted.[8]

Algernon. Oh! there is no use speculating on that subject. Divorces are made in Heaven— [*Jack puts out his hand to take a sandwich. Algernon at once interferes.*] Please don't touch the cucumber sandwiches. They are ordered specially for Aunt Augusta. [*Takes one and eats it.*]

Jack. Well, you have been eating them all the time.

Algernon. That is quite a different matter. She is my aunt. [*Takes plate from below.*] Have some bread and butter. The bread and butter is for Gwendolen. Gwendolen is devoted to bread and butter.

Jack. [*Advancing to table and helping himself.*] And very good bread and butter it is too.

Algernon. Well, my dear fellow, you need not eat as if you were going to eat it all. You behave as if you were married to her already. You are not married to her already, and I don't think you ever will be.

Jack. Why on earth do you say that?

Algernon. Well, in the first place girls never marry the men they flirt with. Girls don't think it right.

9. Algernon's flat acquired a smoking-room in 1899: in earlier texts, Jack has left his cigarette case in "the hall."

10. Like Wilde himself, Jack is a cigarette smoker, much preoccupied with the paraphernalia of cigarette smoking. In the 1890s, cigarettes emerged as an important symbol of both modernity and sexual dissidence, proving an important fashion accessory among gay men and "new" women. Wilde frequently gave specially inscribed cigarette cases as gifts to young men, confessing in court, "I have a weakness for presenting my acquaintances with cigarette cases," and contending that the habit was "less extravagant than giving jeweled garters to women" (H. Montgomery Hyde, *The Trials of Oscar Wilde* [1962; repr., New York: Dover, 1973], 204).

11. Headquarters of London's Metropolitan Police.

Jack. Oh, that is nonsense!

Algernon. It isn't. It is a great truth. It accounts for the extraordinary number of bachelors that one sees all over the place. In the second place, I don't give my consent.

Jack. Your consent!

Algernon. My dear fellow, Gwendolen is my first cousin. And before I allow you to marry her, you will have to clear up the whole question of Cecily. [*Rings bell.*]

Jack. Cecily! What on earth do you mean? What do you mean, Algy, by Cecily? I don't know any one of the name of Cecily.

[*Enter Lane.*]

Algernon. Bring me that cigarette case Mr. Worthing left in the smoking-room[9] the last time he dined here.

Lane. Yes, sir. [*Lane goes out.*]

Jack. Do you mean to say you have had my cigarette case all this time?[10] I wish to goodness you had let me know. I have been writing frantic letters to Scotland Yard[11] about it. I was very nearly offering a large reward.

Algernon. Well, I wish you would offer one. I happen to be more than usually hard up.

Jack. There is no good offering a large reward now that the thing is found.

12. Algernon's "ungentlemanly" reading of a "private cigarette case" foreshadows the manner in which Wilde himself was cross-examined about a cigarette case inscribed and given to Alphonse Conway, a young man with whom Wilde had a brief, sexually charged affair at Worthing at the time he began composing *The Importance of Being Earnest.* "Did you give him a cigarette case?" asked Edward Carson before producing the cigarette case in question: "This is the cigarette case you gave him? . . . Did you put this inscription into it 'Alfonso from his friend Oscar Wilde'?" ("On Alfonso Conway," in *The Real Trial of Oscar Wilde,* ed. Merlin Holland [New York: Perennial, 2004], 147).

13. Once-fashionable spa town in Kent, by Wilde's day a place of retirement for the elderly and the infirm, thus possessing an air of unimpeachable respectability.

[*Enter Lane with the cigarette case on a salver. Algernon takes it at once. Lane goes out.*]

Algernon. I think that is rather mean of you, Ernest, I must say. [*Opens case and examines it.*] However, it makes no matter, for, now that I look at the inscription inside, I find that the thing isn't yours after all.

Jack. Of course it's mine. [*Moving to him.*] You have seen me with it a hundred times, and you have no right whatsoever to read what is written inside. It is a very ungentlemanly thing to read a private cigarette case.[12]

Algernon. Oh! it is absurd to have a hard and fast rule about what one should read and what one shouldn't. More than half of modern culture depends on what one shouldn't read.

Jack. I am quite aware of the fact, and I don't propose to discuss modern culture. It isn't the sort of thing one should talk of in private. I simply want my cigarette case back.

Algernon. Yes; but this isn't your cigarette case. This cigarette case is a present from some one of the name of Cecily, and you said you didn't know any one of that name.

Jack. Well, if you want to know, Cecily happens to be my aunt.

Algernon. Your aunt!

Jack. Yes. Charming old lady she is, too. Lives at Tunbridge Wells.[13] Just give it back to me, Algy.

14. Wilde inserted this stage direction in 1899 in order to underscore Jack's annoyance and determination. But he introduced an error, left uncorrected in the first edition, by writing, "Follows Ernest around the room." "Ernest" has been corrected here to "Algernon."

15. The name *Ernest* drives the punning title of the play, with its ironic endorsement of the need for deception. It repeats a pun that also underpins the 1892 volume of poems *Love in Earnest* by the homosexual poet John Gambril Nicholson (London: Elliot Stock, 1892), in which the ballad "Of Boys' Names" ends, "One name can make my pulses bound, / . . . 'Tis Ernest sets my heart a-flame." Ernest was the actual lover of Nicholson, whose work appeared alongside Wilde's in the undergraduate magazine the *Chameleon*, edited by the homosexual writer John Francis Bloxam.

16. Visiting cards, used by Victorians to announce the identity of a person paying a social call. In England, "introductions are sacraments," comments Ralph Waldo Emerson, and if an Englishman gives you "his private address on a card, it is like an avowal of friendship" (Emerson, *English Traits*, vol. 5 of *Collected Works of Ralph Waldo Emerson*, ed. P. Nicoloff et al. [Cambridge, MA: Harvard University Press, 1994], 59). In Act 2, the card that Algernon retains as proof that Jack's name is Ernest will be presented to Cecily on a silver platter.

Algernon. [*Retreating to back of sofa.*] But why does she call herself little Cecily if she is your aunt and lives at Tunbridge Wells? [*Reading.*] "From little Cecily with her fondest love."

Jack. [*Moving to sofa and kneeling upon it.*] My dear fellow, what on earth is there in that? Some aunts are tall, some aunts are not tall. That is a matter that surely an aunt may be allowed to decide for herself. You seem to think that every aunt should be exactly like your aunt! That is absurd! For Heaven's sake give me back my cigarette case. [*Follows Algernon[14] round the room.*]

Algernon. Yes. But why does your aunt call you her uncle? "From little Cecily, with her fondest love to her dear Uncle Jack." There is no objection, I admit, to an aunt being a small aunt, but why an aunt, no matter what her size may be, should call her own nephew her uncle, I can't quite make out. Besides, your name isn't Jack at all; it is Ernest.[15]

Jack. It isn't Ernest; it's Jack.

Algernon. You have always told me it was Ernest. I have introduced you to every one as Ernest. You answer to the name of Ernest. You look as if your name was Ernest. You are the most earnest-looking person I ever saw in my life. It is perfectly absurd your saying that your name isn't Ernest. It's on your cards.[16] Here is one of them. [*Taking it from*

17. "B. 4 The Albany" was "E. 4 The Albany" throughout the first
London and New York productions. This was precisely the residence
of Wilde's friend the homosexual apologist George Ives, in whose
rooms Wilde had met John Francis Bloxam late in 1894. Rooms in the
Albany, a West End apartment building, were traditionally occupied
by bachelors and men living alone. Wilde changed "E. 4" to "B. 4" for
the first edition of 1899.

18. The term *Bunburyist* is of Wilde's own coinage. The passage of the
Criminal Law Amendment Act in 1885, outlawing "gross indecency"
between men, meant that Wilde, like other homosexuals, was forced
henceforth to live a double life, pursuing homosexual relations with
other men in great secrecy. *Bunburying* is a behavior, or way of life, as
much as an identity.

case.] "Mr. Ernest Worthing, B. 4, The Albany."[17] I'll keep this as a proof that your name is Ernest if ever you attempt to deny it to me, or to Gwendolen, or to any one else. [*Puts the card in his pocket.*]

Jack. Well, my name is Ernest in town and Jack in the country, and the cigarette case was given to me in the country.

Algernon. Yes, but that does not account for the fact that your small Aunt Cecily, who lives at Tunbridge Wells, calls you her dear uncle. Come, old boy, you had much better have the thing out at once.

Jack. My dear Algy, you talk exactly as if you were a dentist. It is very vulgar to talk like a dentist when one isn't a dentist. It produces a false impression.

Algernon. Well, that is exactly what dentists always do. Now, go on! Tell me the whole thing. I may mention that I have always suspected you of being a confirmed and secret Bunburyist;[18] and I am quite sure of it now.

Jack. Bunburyist? What on earth do you mean by a Bunburyist?

Algernon. I'll reveal to you the meaning of that incomparable expression as soon as you are kind enough to inform me why you are Ernest in town and Jack in the country.

Jack. Well, produce my cigarette case first.

19. "that you could not possibly appreciate" was added in 1899.

Algernon. Here it is. [*Hands cigarette case.*] Now produce your explanation, and pray make it improbable. [*Sits on sofa.*]

Jack. My dear fellow, there is nothing improbable about my explanation at all. In fact it's perfectly ordinary. Old Mr. Thomas Cardew, who adopted me when I was a little boy, made me in his will guardian to his grand-daughter, Miss Cecily Cardew. Cecily, who addresses me as her uncle from motives of respect that you could not possibly appreciate,[19] lives at my place in the country under the charge of her admirable governess, Miss Prism.

Algernon. Where is that place in the country, by the way?

Jack. That is nothing to you, dear boy. You are not going to be invited . . . I may tell you candidly that the place is not in Shropshire.

Algernon. I suspected that, my dear fellow! I have Bun-buryed all over Shropshire on two separate occasions. Now, go on. Why are you Ernest in town and Jack in the country?

Jack. My dear Algy, I don't know whether you will be able to understand my real motives. You are hardly serious enough. When one is placed in the position of guardian, one has to adopt a very high moral tone on all subjects. It's one's duty to do so. And as a high moral tone can hardly be said to conduce very much to either one's health or one's happiness, in order to get up to town I have always pretended to have a

20. One of numerous attacks on popular journalism in Wilde's works. Wilde's own writings had frequently—and often viciously—been attacked in the daily papers, leading Wilde to write in "The Soul of Man under Socialism," "In old days men had the rack. Now they have the press," and in England, "we allow absolute freedom to the journalist and entirely limit the artist."

21. Willis's, in King Street, adjacent to the theater where *The Importance* was first performed, was one of Victorian London's most fashionable restaurants.

younger brother of the name of Ernest, who lives in the Albany, and gets into the most dreadful scrapes. That, my dear Algy, is the whole truth pure and simple.

Algernon. The truth is rarely pure and never simple. Modern life would be very tedious if it were either, and modern literature a complete impossibility!

Jack. That wouldn't be at all a bad thing.

Algernon. Literary criticism is not your forte, my dear fellow. Don't try it. You should leave that to people who haven't been at a University. They do it so well in the daily papers.[20] What you really are is a Bunburyist. I was quite right in saying you were a Bunburyist. You are one of the most advanced Bunburyists I know.

Jack. What on earth do you mean?

Algernon. You have invented a very useful younger brother called Ernest, in order that you may be able to come up to town as often as you like. I have invented an invaluable permanent invalid called Bunbury, in order that I may be able to go down into the country whenever I choose. Bunbury is perfectly invaluable. If it wasn't for Bunbury's extraordinary bad health, for instance, I wouldn't be able to dine with you at Willis's to-night,[21] for I have been really engaged to Aunt Augusta for more than a week.

Jack. I haven't asked you to dine with me anywhere to-night.

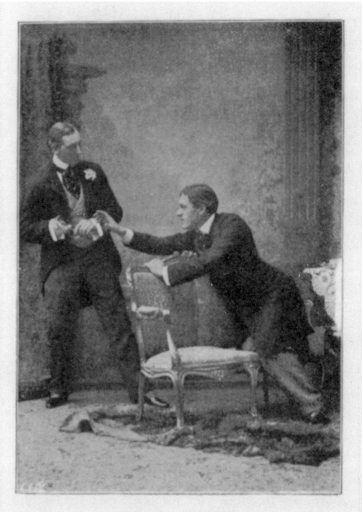

MONCRIEFFE AND WORTHING.

WORTHING : *" Give me back my cigarette-case."*

"Give me back my cigarette case," publicity still from *The Sketch*,
March 20, 1895. Widener Library, Harvard University.

Algernon. I know. You are absurdly careless about sending out invitations. It is very foolish of you. Nothing annoys people so much as not receiving invitations.

Jack. You had much better dine with your Aunt Augusta.

Algernon. I haven't the smallest intention of doing anything of the kind. To begin with, I dined there on Monday, and once a week is quite enough to dine with one's own relations. In the second place, whenever I do dine there I am always treated as a member of the family, and sent down with either no woman at all, or two. In the third place, I know perfectly well whom she will place me next to, to-night. She will place me next Mary Farquhar, who always flirts with her own husband across the dinner-table. That is not very pleasant. Indeed, it is not even decent . . . and that sort of thing is enormously on the increase. The amount of women in London who flirt with their own husbands is perfectly scandalous. It looks so bad. It is simply washing one's clean linen in public. Besides, now that I know you to be a confirmed Bunburyist I naturally want to talk to you about Bunburying. I want to tell you the rules.

Jack. I'm not a Bunburyist at all. If Gwendolen accepts me, I am going to kill my brother, indeed I think I'll kill him in any case. Cecily is a little too much interested in him. It is rather a bore. So I am going to get rid of Ernest. And I strongly advise you to do the same with Mr. . . . with your invalid friend who has the absurd name.

22. The plays of Alexandre Dumas *fils*, Eugène Scribe, and others, while enormously popular in Victorian Britain, were considered risqué by virtue of their frank presentation of sexual desire. Wilde had himself written a "corrupt French Drama": his play *Salomé*, depicting the insatiable, murderous desire of Salomé for Iokanaan, as well as of the married Herod for his stepdaughter, had originally been written in French and had been banned by the British Censor in 1892.

23. That Algernon's flat possesses an electric doorbell is a sign of how modern and up-to-date it is. In draft and rehearsal copies, the stage directions indicate merely "bell" or "a ring."

24. One of many witticisms added for the 1899 edition. Wilde tried "angry" and "argumentative" before settling on the "Wagnerian" manner of Lady Bracknell's ring. The operas of Richard Wagner were much in vogue in the 1890s, though here Wilde's joke turns on the perceived loudness and ferocity of Wagner's music. As Lady Victoria Wotton wittily says of Wagner's music in *Dorian Gray*, "it is so loud that one can talk the whole time, without other people hearing what one says" (*The Picture of Dorian Gray: An Annotated Uncensored Edition*, ed. Nicholas Frankel [Cambridge, MA: Harvard University Press, 2011], 113).

Algernon. Nothing will induce me to part with Bunbury, and if you ever get married, which seems to me extremely problematic, you will be very glad to know Bunbury. A man who marries without knowing Bunbury has a very tedious time of it.

Jack. That is nonsense. If I marry a charming girl like Gwendolen, and she is the only girl I ever saw in my life that I would marry, I certainly won't want to know Bunbury.

Algernon. Then your wife will. You don't seem to realise, that in married life three is company and two is none.

Jack. [*Sententiously.*] That, my dear young friend, is the theory that the corrupt French Drama has been propounding for the last fifty years.[22]

Algernon. Yes; and that the happy English home has proved in half the time.

Jack. For heaven's sake, don't try to be cynical. It's perfectly easy to be cynical.

Algernon. My dear fellow, it isn't easy to be anything nowadays. There's such a lot of beastly competition about. [*The sound of an electric bell is heard.*][23] Ah! that must be Aunt Augusta. Only relatives, or creditors, ever ring in that Wagnerian manner.[24] Now, if I get her out of the way for ten minutes, so that you can have an opportunity for proposing to Gwendolen, may I dine with you to-night at Willis's?

25. Wilde himself was "serious about meals," writing wittily that the New York restaurant Delmonico's has "done more to promote a good feeling between England and America than anything else has in this century" and that "the British cook is a foolish woman who should be turned, for her iniquities, into a pillar of that salt which she never knows how to use" ("Dinners and Dishes," *Pall Mall Gazette*, 7 Mar. 1885, repr. in *Journalism: Part One*, vol. 6 of *The Complete Works of Oscar Wilde*, ed. John Stokes and Mark W. Turner [Oxford: Oxford University Press, 2013] 39–40).

26. "In fact the two things rarely go together" was added in 1899.

27. Lady Bracknell's bow of "icy coldness," introduced in 1899 as a replacement for the more neutral greeting "Good afternoon, Mr. Worthing," is motivated by disapproval. She is evidently aware already of Jack's courtship of her daughter, even though he is "not down on [her] list of eligible young men," as she later puts it.

28. This witty speech was added in 1899.

Jack. I suppose so, if you want to.

Algernon. Yes, but you must be serious about it. I hate people who are not serious about meals. It is so shallow of them.[25]

[*Enter Lane.*]

Lane. Lady Bracknell and Miss Fairfax.

[*Algernon goes forward to meet them. Enter Lady Bracknell and Gwendolen.*]

Lady Bracknell. Good afternoon, dear Algernon, I hope you are behaving very well.

Algernon. I'm feeling very well, Aunt Augusta.

Lady Bracknell. That's not quite the same thing. In fact the two things rarely go together.[26] [*Sees Jack and bows to him with icy coldness.*][27]

Algernon. [*To Gwendolen.*] Dear me, you are smart!

Gwendolen. I am always smart! Aren't I, Mr. Worthing?

Jack. You're quite perfect, Miss Fairfax.

Gwendolen. Oh! I hope I am not that. It would leave no room for developments, and I intend to develop in many directions.[28] [*Gwendolen and Jack sit down together in the corner.*]

Lady Bracknell. I'm sorry if we are a little late, Algernon, but I was obliged to call on dear Lady Harbury. I hadn't been there since her poor husband's death. I never saw a

29. In 1899, Wilde underscored Algernon's feigned disappointment at the lack of cucumbers by adding this speech as well as the previous four lines of dialogue running from "No cucumbers!"

woman so altered; she looks quite twenty years younger. And now I'll have a cup of tea, and one of those nice cucumber sandwiches you promised me.

Algernon. Certainly, Aunt Augusta. [*Goes over to tea-table.*]

Lady Bracknell. Won't you come and sit here, Gwendolen?

Gwendolen. Thanks, mamma, I'm quite comfortable where I am.

Algernon. [*Picking up empty plate in horror.*] Good heavens! Lane! Why are there no cucumber sandwiches? I ordered them specially.

Lane. [*Gravely.*] There were no cucumbers in the market this morning, sir. I went down twice.

Algernon. No cucumbers!

Lane. No, sir. Not even for ready money.

Algernon. That will do, Lane, thank you.

Lane. Thank you, sir. [*Goes out.*]

Algernon. I am greatly distressed, Aunt Augusta, about there being no cucumbers, not even for ready money.[29]

Lady Bracknell. It really makes no matter, Algernon. I had some crumpets with Lady Harbury, who seems to me to be living entirely for pleasure now.

Algernon. I hear her hair has turned quite gold from grief.

30. "and, I need hardly say, a terrible disappointment to me" was added in 1899.

Lady Bracknell. It certainly has changed its colour. From what cause I, of course, cannot say. [*Algernon crosses and hands tea.*] Thank you. I've quite a treat for you to-night, Algernon. I am going to send you down with Mary Farquhar. She is such a nice woman, and so attentive to her husband. It's delightful to watch them.

Algernon. I am afraid, Aunt Augusta, I shall have to give up the pleasure of dining with you to-night after all.

Lady Bracknell. [*Frowning.*] I hope not, Algernon. It would put my table completely out. Your uncle would have to dine upstairs. Fortunately he is accustomed to that.

Algernon. It is a great bore, and, I need hardly say, a terrible disappointment to me,[30] but the fact is I have just had a telegram to say that my poor friend Bunbury is very ill again. [*Exchanges glances with Jack.*] They seem to think I should be with him.

Lady Bracknell. It is very strange. This Mr. Bunbury seems to suffer from curiously bad health.

Algernon. Yes; poor Bunbury is a dreadful invalid.

Lady Bracknell. Well, I must say, Algernon, that I think it is high time that Mr. Bunbury made up his mind whether he was going to live or to die. This shilly-shallying with the question is absurd. Nor do I in any way approve of the modern sympathy with invalids. I consider it morbid. Illness of any kind is hardly a thing to be encouraged in others. Health is

31. "which, in most cases, was probably not much" was added in 1899.

32. "if he is still conscious" was added in 1899.

the primary duty of life. I am always telling that to your poor uncle, but he never seems to take much notice . . . as far as any improvement in his ailment goes. I should be much obliged if you would ask Mr. Bunbury, from me, to be kind enough not to have a relapse on Saturday, for I rely on you to arrange my music for me. It is my last reception, and one wants something that will encourage conversation, particularly at the end of the season when every one has practically said whatever they had to say, which, in most cases, was probably not much.[31]

Algernon. I'll speak to Bunbury, Aunt Augusta, if he is still conscious,[32] and I think I can promise you he'll be all right by Saturday. Of course the music is a great difficulty. You see, if one plays good music, people don't listen, and if one plays bad music people don't talk. But I'll run over the programme I've drawn out, if you will kindly come into the next room for a moment.

Lady Bracknell. Thank you, Algernon. It is very thoughtful of you. [*Rising, and following Algernon.*] I'm sure the programme will be delightful, after a few expurgations. French songs I cannot possibly allow. People always seem to think that they are improper, and either look shocked, which is vulgar, or laugh, which is worse. But German sounds a thoroughly respectable language, and indeed, I believe, is so. Gwendolen, you will accompany me.

Gwendolen. Certainly, mamma.

33. Algernon's flat acquired its music-room in 1899. Before this date, the stage direction read merely, "Exit Lady B. with Algernon, leaving door open."

34. "In fact, I am never wrong" was added in 1899.

[*Lady Bracknell and Algernon go into the music-room,*[33] *Gwendolen remains behind.*]

Jack. Charming day it has been, Miss Fairfax.

Gwendolen. Pray don't talk to me about the weather, Mr. Worthing. Whenever people talk to me about the weather, I always feel quite certain that they mean something else. And that makes me so nervous.

Jack. I do mean something else.

Gwendolen. I thought so. In fact, I am never wrong.[34]

Jack. And I would like to be allowed to take advantage of Lady Bracknell's temporary absence . . .

Gwendolen. I would certainly advise you to do so. Mamma has a way of coming back suddenly into a room that I have often had to speak to her about.

Jack. [*Nervously.*] Miss Fairfax, ever since I met you I have admired you more than any girl . . . I have ever met since . . . I met you.

Gwendolen. Yes, I am quite well aware of the fact. And I often wish that in public, at any rate, you had been more demonstrative. For me you have always had an irresistible fascination. Even before I met you I was far from indifferent to you. [*Jack looks at her in amazement.*] We live, as I hope you know, Mr. Worthing, in an age of ideals. The fact is constantly mentioned in the more expensive monthly

35. "and has reached the provincial pulpits, I am told" was added in 1899.

36. Mrs. Allonby, in Wilde's play *A Woman of No Importance*, is married to a man named Ernest, who possesses "a very strong, ... square chin," who is "invariably calm," and who spoke only what was "perfect true" when, before marrying his fiancée, he told her "on his knees that he had never loved any one before in the whole course of his life." But Mrs. Allonby is now "horribly deceived in Ernest," whom she considers "a sort of promissory note" (Act Two, *A Woman of No Importance*, in *Complete Works of Oscar Wilde*, ed. Merlin Holland, rev. ed. [London: Harper Collins, 1994], 479–80).

magazines, and has reached the provincial pulpits, I am told;[35] and my ideal has always been to love some one of the name of Ernest. There is something in that name that inspires absolute confidence.[36] The moment Algernon first mentioned to me that he had a friend called Ernest, I knew I was destined to love you.

Jack. You really love me, Gwendolen?

Gwendolen. Passionately!

Jack. Darling! You don't know how happy you've made me.

Gwendolen. My own Ernest!

Jack. But you don't really mean to say that you couldn't love me if my name wasn't Ernest?

Gwendolen. But your name is Ernest.

Jack. Yes, I know it is. But supposing it was something else? Do you mean to say you couldn't love me then?

Gwendolen. [*Glibly.*] Ah! that is clearly a metaphysical speculation, and like most metaphysical speculations has very little reference at all to the actual facts of real life, as we know them.

Jack. Personally, darling, to speak quite candidly, I don't much care about the name of Ernest . . . I don't think the name suits me at all.

37. Wilde is mocking popular late-Victorian theories of interpersonal psychology, which posited that influence results from a transference of physical energy producing a physiological sensation: "Why do we feel in the presence of some persons that persuasive warmth which makes their society alluring?" asked the *Psychical Review* in 1894: "Is it not true that the radiating brain vibrations are . . . harmonious?" (*Psychical Review* 2 [1894]: 256).

Gwendolen. It suits you perfectly. It is a divine name. It has a music of its own. It produces vibrations.

Jack. Well, really, Gwendolen, I must say that I think there are lots of other much nicer names. I think Jack, for instance, a charming name.

Gwendolen. Jack? . . . No, there is very little music in the name Jack, if any at all, indeed. It does not thrill. It produces absolutely no vibrations[37] . . . I have known several Jacks, and they all, without exception, were more than usually plain. Besides, Jack is a notorious domesticity for John! And I pity any woman who is married to a man called John. She would probably never be allowed to know the entrancing pleasure of a single moment's solitude. The only really safe name is Ernest.

Jack. Gwendolen, I must get christened at once—I mean we must get married at once. There is no time to be lost.

Gwendolen. Married, Mr. Worthing?

Jack. [*Astounded.*] Well . . . surely. You know that I love you, and you led me to believe, Miss Fairfax, that you were not absolutely indifferent to me.

Gwendolen. I adore you. But you haven't proposed to me yet. Nothing has been said at all about marriage. The subject has not even been touched on.

Jack. Well . . . may I propose to you now?

Gwendolen. I think it would be an admirable opportunity. And to spare you any possible disappointment, Mr. Worthing, I think it only fair to tell you quite frankly before-hand that I am fully determined to accept you.

Jack. Gwendolen!

Gwendolen. Yes, Mr. Worthing, what have you got to say to me?

Jack. You know what I have got to say to you.

Gwendolen. Yes, but you don't say it.

Jack. Gwendolen, will you marry me? [*Goes on his knees.*]

Gwendolen. Of course I will, darling. How long you have been about it! I am afraid you have had very little experience in how to propose.

Jack. My own one, I have never loved any one in the world but you.

Gwendolen. Yes, but men often propose for practice. I know my brother Gerald does. All my girl-friends tell me so. What wonderfully blue eyes you have, Ernest! They are quite, quite, blue. I hope you will always look at me just like that, especially when there are other people present. [*Enter Lady Bracknell.*]

Lady Bracknell. Mr. Worthing! Rise, sir, from this semi-recumbent posture. It is most indecorous.

38. Before Wilde could marry his future wife, Constance, her grand-father and guardian, John Horatio Lloyd, was determined "to put one or two questions" to him, and "only when Oscar could answer these points would Constance's grandfather 'give a considered consent'" (Franny Moyle, *Constance: The Tragic and Scandalous Life of Mrs. Oscar Wilde* [London: John Murray, 2011], 76).

Gwendolen. Mamma! [*He tries to rise; she restrains him.*] I must beg you to retire. This is no place for you. Besides, Mr. Worthing has not quite finished yet.

Lady Bracknell. Finished what, may I ask?

Gwendolen. I am engaged to Mr. Worthing, mamma. [*They rise together.*]

Lady Bracknell. Pardon me, you are not engaged to any one. When you do become engaged to some one, I, or your father, should his health permit him, will inform you of the fact. An engagement should come on a young girl as a surprise, pleasant or unpleasant, as the case may be. It is hardly a matter that she could be allowed to arrange for herself . . . And now I have a few questions to put to you, Mr. Worthing.[38] While I am making these inquiries, you, Gwendolen, will wait for me below in the carriage.

Gwendolen. [*Reproachfully.*] Mamma!

Lady Bracknell. In the carriage, Gwendolen! [*Gwendolen goes to the door. She and Jack blow kisses to each other behind Lady Bracknell's back. Lady Bracknell looks vaguely about as if she could not understand what the noise was. Finally turns round.*] Gwendolen, the carriage!

Gwendolen. Yes, mamma. [*Goes out, looking back at Jack.*]

Lady Bracknell. [*Sitting down.*] You can take a seat, Mr. Worthing. [*Looks in her pocket for note-book and pencil.*]

39. Altered from "twenty-five" in the first manuscript draft. In later productions, George Alexander altered Jack's age to thirty-five—as Russell Jackson observes, Alexander was thirty-six when he first performed the role of Jack.

Jack. Thank you, Lady Bracknell, I prefer standing.

Lady Bracknell. [*Pencil and note-book in hand.*] I feel bound to tell you that you are not down on my list of eligible young men, although I have the same list as the dear Duchess of Bolton has. We work together, in fact. However, I am quite ready to enter your name, should your answers be what a really affectionate mother requires. Do you smoke?

Jack. Well, yes, I must admit I smoke.

Lady Bracknell. I am glad to hear it. A man should always have an occupation of some kind. There are far too many idle men in London as it is. How old are you?

Jack. Twenty-nine.[39]

Lady Bracknell. A very good age to be married at. I have always been of opinion that a man who desires to get married should know either everything or nothing. Which do you know?

Jack. [*After some hesitation.*] I know nothing, Lady Bracknell.

Lady Bracknell. I am pleased to hear it. I do not approve of anything that tampers with natural ignorance. Ignorance is like a delicate exotic fruit; touch it and the bloom is gone. The whole theory of modern education is radically unsound. Fortunately in England, at any rate, education produces no effect whatsoever. If it did, it would prove a

40. Wilde added this witticism in 1899, initially by adding from "If it did" to "acts of violence," then later adding "in Grosvenor Square." Grosvenor Square, in London's Mayfair district, is where Lord Henry Wotton resides in *The Picture of Dorian Gray*. Bordered on each side by expensive mansions, it was in Wilde's day the most exclusive and aristocratic of London addresses.

41. An extremely high income for the 1890s, placing Jack among England's very wealthiest.

42. A topical reference to the introduction in 1894 of so-called death duties or estate duties, which taxed large estates by as much as 8 percent upon the owner's death.

43. The witty final sentence of this speech was added in 1899.

44. Another of London's most prestigious and aristocratic addresses.

serious danger to the upper classes, and probably lead to acts of violence in Grosvenor Square.[40] What is your income?

Jack. Between seven and eight thousand a year.[41]

Lady Bracknell. [*Makes a note in her book.*] In land, or in investments?

Jack. In investments, chiefly.

Lady Bracknell. That is satisfactory. What between the duties expected of one during one's lifetime, and the duties exacted from one after one's death,[42] land has ceased to be either a profit or a pleasure. It gives one position, and prevents one from keeping it up. That's all that can be said about land.

Jack. I have a country house with some land, of course, attached to it, about fifteen hundred acres, I believe; but I don't depend on that for my real income. In fact, as far as I can make out, the poachers are the only people who make anything out of it.[43]

Lady Bracknell. A country house! How many bedrooms? Well, that point can be cleared up afterwards. You have a town house, I hope? A girl with a simple, unspoiled nature, like Gwendolen, could hardly be expected to reside in the country.

Jack. Well, I own a house in Belgrave Square,[44] but it is let by the year to Lady Bloxham. Of course, I can get it back whenever I like, at six months' notice.

45. The Liberal Unionist Party was formed in 1886 by a faction that broke away from the Liberal Party when its leader, William Ewart Gladstone, affiliated his party with support for Irish Home Rule. Lady Bracknell's following comment that "they count as Tories" is prescient: although the Liberal Unionists had been strongly allied with the Conservative Party ("Tories") since their formation, they created a coalition government with the Tories in the summer of 1895, shortly after *The Importance of Being Earnest* was first produced, and seventeen years later were formally merged with the Tories.

46. Lady Bracknell is distinguishing between the intimate dinner party and the more formal evening party, to which a diverse variety of acquaintances might be invited. Liberal Unionists are more likely to be found at the latter, she implies.

47. Many readers prefer the earlier version of this famous witticism ("To lose one parent may be regarded as a misfortune . . . to lose both looks like carelessness"), which had appeared in prepublication texts of the play and which Robert Ross reinstated when editing the 1908 *Complete Works of Oscar Wilde*, 14 vols. (London: Methuen, 1908). But Wilde shortened it to its present form in preparing the 1899 edition.

Lady Bracknell. Lady Bloxham? I don't know her.

Jack. Oh, she goes about very little. She is a lady considerably advanced in years.

Lady Bracknell. Ah, nowadays that is no guarantee of respectability of character. What number in Belgrave Square?

Jack. 149.

Lady Bracknell. [*Shaking her head.*] The unfashionable side. I thought there was something. However, that could easily be altered.

Jack. Do you mean the fashion, or the side?

Lady Bracknell. [*Sternly.*] Both, if necessary, I presume. What are your politics?

Jack. Well, I am afraid I really have none. I am a Liberal Unionist.[45]

Lady Bracknell. Oh, they count as Tories. They dine with us. Or come in the evening,[46] at any rate. Now to minor matters. Are your parents living?

Jack. I have lost both my parents.

Lady Bracknell. Both? . . . That seems like carelessness.[47] Who was your father? He was evidently a man of some wealth. Was he born in what the Radical papers call the

48. Lady Bracknell's question was originally more direct: "Was he born in the purple of commerce, or did he rise from the ranks of the aristocracy?" But in preparing the 1899 edition, Wilde revised it to make it more politically pointed, first adding "what we must call" before settling on "what the Radical papers call."

49. Lady Bracknell is one of the most treasured roles for actresses in English theater, though increasingly the role attracts male actors interested by elements of androgyny or masculinity in Wilde's characterization of her. Judi Dench, Joan Plowright, and Maggie Smith have all performed the role with great distinction, although Edith Evans's performances—immortalized in Anthony Asquith's great film production of 1952—remain *the* touchstone for many people. What has wittily been called Evans's "thirty-six-syllable" inflection of the three-syllable question "A hand-bag?" (David Woods, quoted in Maddy Costa, "Handbags at Dawn," *The Guardian,* 22 Jan. 2008)—a glissando descending from the topmost to the bottommost registers of Evans's voice—"sits like a monkey on the shoulder" of modern actresses performing the role, says the actress Penelope Keith (quoted in "Handbags at Dawn").

50. "or Thomas" was added in 1899.

purple of commerce,[48] or did he rise from the ranks of the aristocracy?

Jack. I am afraid I really don't know. The fact is, Lady Bracknell, I said I had lost my parents. It would be nearer the truth to say that my parents seem to have lost me . . . I don't actually know who I am by birth. I was . . . well, I was found.

Lady Bracknell. Found!

Jack. The late Mr. Thomas Cardew, an old gentleman of a very charitable and kindly disposition, found me, and gave me the name of Worthing, because he happened to have a first-class ticket for Worthing in his pocket at the time. Worthing is a place in Sussex. It is a seaside resort.

Lady Bracknell. Where did the charitable gentleman who had a first-class ticket for this seaside resort find you?

Jack. [*Gravely.*] In a hand-bag.

Lady Bracknell. A hand-bag?[49]

Jack. [*Very seriously.*] Yes, Lady Bracknell. I was in a hand-bag—a somewhat large, black leather hand-bag, with handles to it—an ordinary hand-bag in fact.

Lady Bracknell. In what locality did this Mr. James, or Thomas,[50] Cardew come across this ordinary hand-bag?

Jack. In the cloak-room at Victoria Station. It was given to him in mistake for his own.

Lady Bracknell. The cloak-room at Victoria Station?

Jack. Yes. The Brighton line.

Lady Bracknell. The line is immaterial. Mr. Worthing, I confess I feel somewhat bewildered by what you have just told me. To be born, or at any rate bred, in a hand-bag, whether it had handles or not, seems to me to display a contempt for the ordinary decencies of family life that reminds one of the worst excesses of the French Revolution. And I presume you know what that unfortunate movement led to? As for the particular locality in which the hand-bag was found, a cloak-room at a railway station might serve to conceal a social indiscretion—has probably, indeed, been used for that purpose before now—but it could hardly be regarded as an assured basis for a recognised position in good society.

Jack. May I ask you then what you would advise me to do? I need hardly say I would do anything in the world to ensure Gwendolen's happiness.

Lady Bracknell. I would strongly advise you, Mr. Worthing, to try and acquire some relations as soon as possible, and to make a definite effort to produce at any rate one parent, of either sex, before the season is quite over.

Jack. Well, I don't see how I could possibly manage to do that. I can produce the hand-bag at any moment. It is in my dressing-room at home. I really think that should satisfy you, Lady Bracknell.

51. The last three sentences of this speech, from "I know" to "ill-natured of her," were added in 1899.

52. Lady Bracknell echoes many characteristics of Wilde's own mother, the indomitable Lady Wilde. "Never before, nor since, have I met a women who was so absolutely sure of herself," wrote Anna de Brémont of Lady Wilde, fifteen years after the latter's death: she was "intensely earnest" (de Brémont, *Oscar Wilde and His Mother* [London: Everett, 1911], 47–48). Many years later, Wilde's son Vyvyan Holland recalled his grandmother as "a terrifying and very severe old lady" and confessed that, when small, "I protested strongly every time I was taken to pay her a duty visit" (Holland, *Son of Oscar Wilde* [1954; repr., Oxford: Oxford University Press, 1987], 24).

Lady Bracknell. Me, sir! What has it to do with me? You can hardly imagine that I and Lord Bracknell would dream of allowing our only daughter—a girl brought up with the utmost care—to marry into a cloak-room, and form an alliance with a parcel? Good morning, Mr. Worthing!

[*Lady Bracknell sweeps out in majestic indignation.*]

Jack. Good morning! [*Algernon, from the other room, strikes up the Wedding March. Jack looks perfectly furious, and goes to the door.*] For goodness' sake don't play that ghastly tune, Algy. How idiotic you are!

[*The music stops and Algernon enters cheerily.*]

Algernon. Didn't it go off all right, old boy? You don't mean to say Gwendolen refused you? I know it is a way she has. She is always refusing people. I think it is most ill-natured of her.[51]

Jack. Oh, Gwendolen is as right as a trivet. As far as she is concerned, we are engaged. Her mother is perfectly unbearable. Never met such a Gorgon . . . I don't really know what a Gorgon is like, but I am quite sure that Lady Bracknell is one.[52] In any case, she is a monster, without being a myth, which is rather unfair . . . I beg your pardon, Algy, I suppose I shouldn't talk about your own aunt in that way before you.

Algernon. My dear boy, I love hearing my relations abused. It is the only thing that makes me put up with them at all.

53. In "Phrases and Philosophies for the Use of the Young" (*The Chameleon*, December 1894), Wilde observes that "the well-bred contradict other people. The wise contradict themselves."

Relations are simply a tedious pack of people, who haven't got the remotest knowledge of how to live, nor the smallest instinct about when to die.

Jack. Oh, that is nonsense!

Algernon. It isn't!

Jack. Well, I won't argue about the matter. You always want to argue about things.

Algernon. That is exactly what things were originally made for.[53]

Jack. Upon my word, if I thought that, I'd shoot myself . . . [*A pause.*] You don't think there is any chance of Gwendolen becoming like her mother in about a hundred and fifty years, do you, Algy?

Algernon. All women become like their mothers. That is their tragedy. No man does. That's his.

Jack. Is that clever?

Algernon. It is perfectly phrased! and quite as true as any observation in civilized life should be.

Jack. I am sick to death of cleverness. Everybody is clever nowadays. You can't go anywhere without meeting clever people. The thing has become an absolute public nuisance. I wish to goodness we had a few fools left.

Algernon. We have.

54. "If one tells the truth," Wilde observes in "Phrases and Philosophies for the Use of the Young" (*The Chameleon*, December 1894), "one is sure, sooner or later, to be found out."

Jack. I should extremely like to meet them. What do they talk about?

Algernon. The fools? Oh! about the clever people, of course.

Jack. What fools!

Algernon. By the way, did you tell Gwendolen the truth about your being Ernest in town, and Jack in the country?

Jack. [*In a very patronising manner.*] My dear fellow, the truth isn't quite the sort of thing one tells to a nice, sweet, refined girl.[54] What extraordinary ideas you have about the way to behave to a woman!

Algernon. The only way to behave to a woman is to make love to her, if she is pretty, and to some one else if she is plain.

Jack. Oh, that is nonsense.

Algernon. What about your brother? What about the profligate Ernest?

Jack. Oh, before the end of the week I shall have got rid of him. I'll say he died in Paris of apoplexy. Lots of people die of apoplexy, quite suddenly, don't they?

Algernon. Yes, but it's hereditary, my dear fellow. It's a sort of thing that runs in families. You had much better say a severe chill.

Jack. You are sure a severe chill isn't hereditary, or anything of that kind?

Algernon. Of course it isn't!

Jack. Very well, then. My poor brother Ernest is carried off suddenly in Paris, by a severe chill. That gets rid of him.

Algernon. But I thought you said that . . . Miss Cardew was a little too much interested in your poor brother Ernest? Won't she feel his loss a good deal?

Jack. Oh, that is all right. Cecily is not a silly romantic girl, I am glad to say. She has got a capital appetite, goes long walks, and pays no attention at all to her lessons.

Algernon. I would rather like to see Cecily.

Jack. I will take very good care you never do. She is excessively pretty, and she is only just eighteen.

Algernon. Have you told Gwendolen yet that you have an excessively pretty ward who is only just eighteen?

Jack. Oh! one doesn't blurt these things out to people. Cecily and Gwendolen are perfectly certain to be extremely great friends. I'll bet you anything you like that half an hour after they have met, they will be calling each other sister.

Algernon. Women only do that when they have called each other a lot of other things first. Now, my dear boy, if we want

55. The Empire Theatre of Varieties, in Leicester Square, one of London's best known and most popular music halls. It was known for its spectacular ballets as well as its ornate raised "Promenade" at the back of the stalls, a notorious rendezvous for prostitutes and raffish young men-about-town. See John Stokes, "'Prudes on the Prowl': The View from the Empire Promenade," in *In the Nineties* [Chicago: University of Chicago Press, 1989], 53–94.

to get a good table at Willis's, we really must go and dress. Do you know it is nearly seven?

Jack. [*Irritably.*] Oh! It always is nearly seven.

Algernon. Well, I'm hungry.

Jack. I never knew you when you weren't . . .

Algernon. What shall we do after dinner? Go to a theatre?

Jack. Oh no! I loathe listening.

Algernon. Well, let us go to the Club?

Jack. Oh, no! I hate talking.

Algernon. Well, we might trot round to the Empire at ten?[55]

Jack. Oh, no! I can't bear looking at things. It is so silly.

Algernon. Well, what shall we do?

Jack. Nothing!

Algernon. It is awfully hard work doing nothing. However, I don't mind hard work where there is no definite object of any kind.

[*Enter Lane.*]

Lane. Miss Fairfax.

[*Enter Gwendolen. Lane goes out.*]

Algernon. Gwendolen, upon my word!

56. Gwendolen's fearlessness at the prospect of multiple marriages—and presumably divorces—is something she shares with modern Americans, according to Wilde, who had once written, "The American man marries early, and the American woman marries often" ("The American Man," *Court and Society Review*, 13 Apr. 1887, repr. in *Journalism: Part One*, vol. 6 of *The Complete Works of Oscar Wilde*, ed. John Stokes and Mark W. Turner [Oxford: Oxford University Press, 2013], 143).

Gwendolen. Algy, kindly turn your back. I have something very particular to say to Mr. Worthing.

Algernon. Really, Gwendolen, I don't think I can allow this at all.

Gwendolen. Algy, you always adopt a strictly immoral attitude towards life. You are not quite old enough to do that. [*Algernon retires to the fireplace.*]

Jack. My own darling!

Gwendolen. Ernest, we may never be married. From the expression on mamma's face I fear we never shall. Few parents nowadays pay any regard to what their children say to them. The old-fashioned respect for the young is fast dying out. Whatever influence I ever had over mamma, I lost at the age of three. But although she may prevent us from becoming man and wife, and I may marry some one else, and marry often,[56] nothing that she can possibly do can alter my eternal devotion to you.

Jack. Dear Gwendolen!

Gwendolen. The story of your romantic origin, as related to me by mamma, with unpleasing comments, has naturally stirred the deeper fibres of my nature. Your Christian name has an irresistible fascination. The simplicity of your character makes you exquisitely incomprehensible to me. Your town address at the Albany I have. What is your address in the country?

57. Like shirt collars, shirt cuffs were highly starched; and like Wilde, Algernon evidently takes great pride in his cuffs: he will later say, "I can't eat muffins in an agitated manner. The butter would probably get on my cuffs."

58. *"after looking at the envelopes"* was added in 1899.

Jack. The Manor House, Woolton, Hertfordshire.

[*Algernon, who has been carefully listening, smiles to himself, and writes the address on his shirt-cuff.*[57] *Then picks up the Railway Guide.*]

Gwendolen. There is a good postal service, I suppose? It may be necessary to do something desperate. That of course will require serious consideration. I will communicate with you daily.

Jack. My own one!

Gwendolen. How long do you remain in town?

Jack. Till Monday.

Gwendolen. Good! Algy, you may turn round now.

Algernon. Thanks, I've turned round already.

Gwendolen. You may also ring the bell.

Jack. You will let me see you to your carriage, my own darling?

Gwendolen. Certainly.

Jack. [*To Lane, who now enters.*] I will see Miss Fairfax out.

Lane. Yes, sir. [*Jack and Gwendolen go off. Lane presents several letters on a salver to Algernon. It is to be surmised that they are bills, as Algernon, after looking at the envelopes,*[58] *tears them up.*]

MONCRIEFFE AND LANE, HIS SERVANT (MR. KINSEY PEILE).

MONCRIEFFE : "*Lane, you're a perfect pessimist!*"
LANE : "*I do my best to give satisfaction.*"

"Lane, you're a perfect pessimist," publicity still from *The Sketch*, March 20, 1895. Widener Library, Harvard University.

Algernon. A glass of sherry, Lane.

Lane. Yes, sir.

Algernon. To-morrow, Lane, I'm going Bunburying.

Lane. Yes, sir.

Algernon. I shall probably not be back till Monday. You can put up my dress clothes, my smoking jacket, and all the Bunbury suits . . .

Lane. Yes, sir. [*Handing sherry.*]

Algernon. I hope to-morrow will be a fine day, Lane.

Lane. It never is, sir.

Algernon. Lane, you're a perfect pessimist.

Lane. I do my best to give satisfaction, sir.

[*Enter Jack. Lane goes off.*]

Jack. There's a sensible, intellectual girl! the only girl I ever cared for in my life. [*Algernon is laughing immoderately.*] What on earth are you so amused at?

Algernon. Oh, I'm a little anxious about poor Bunbury, that is all.

Jack. If you don't take care, your friend Bunbury will get you into a serious scrape some day.

59. This important stage direction was added only in 1899.

Algernon. I love scrapes. They are the only things that are never serious.

Jack. Oh, that's nonsense, Algy. You never talk anything but nonsense.

Algernon. Nobody ever does. [*Jack looks indignantly at him, and leaves the room. Algernon lights a cigarette, reads his shirt-cuff, and smiles.*][59]

ACT-DROP

1. The gardener Moulton was originally a character in the play, given dialogue of his own, but at Alexander's urging, Wilde cut him, possibly to save on an actor's salary, when reducing the play from four to three acts.

2. Miss Prism combines an interest in German with (as we are later told) a desire to be a novelist. A number of prominent Victorian women writers began their careers by translating works from the German, a practice that Susanne Stark describes as "a courageous, though at times camouflaged, move into the realm of literary professionalism" (Stark, *"Behind Inverted Commas": Translation and Anglo-German Cultural Relations* [Clevedon, UK: Multilingual Matters, 1999], 45). Wilde's own mother was a skilled German translator (she translated works by Wilhelm Meinhold and Marie Schwab), but her example evidently had little effect on Wilde personally: "I am going to take up the study of German," Wilde remarked in a letter from Reading prison in 1896; "indeed this seems to be the proper place for such a study" (Wilde to Robert Ross, Nov. 1896, in *Complete Letters of Oscar Wilde*, ed. Merlin Holland and Rupert Hart-Davis [New York: Henry Holt, 2000], 669).

3. "Indeed, he always lays stress on your German when he is leaving for town" was added in 1899. Jack stresses Cecily's German doubtless because, as Lady Bracknell earlier put it, "German sounds a thoroughly respectable language."

ACT TWO

SCENE: Garden at the Manor House. A flight of grey stone steps leads up to the house. The garden, an old-fashioned one, full of roses. Time of year, July. Basket chairs, and a table covered with books, are set under a large yew-tree. Miss Prism discovered seated at the table. Cecily is at the back watering flowers.

Miss Prism. [*Calling.*] Cecily, Cecily! Surely such a utilitarian occupation as the watering of flowers is rather Moulton's duty than yours?[1] Especially at a moment when intellectual pleasures await you. Your German grammar is on the table. Pray open it at page fifteen. We will repeat yesterday's lesson.[2]

Cecily. [*Coming over very slowly.*] But I don't like German. It isn't at all a becoming language. I know perfectly well that I look quite plain after my German lesson.

Miss Prism. Child, you know how anxious your guardian is that you should improve yourself in every way. He laid particular stress on your German, as he was leaving for town yesterday. Indeed, he always lays stress on your German when he is leaving for town.[3]

4. Prior to 1899, Cecily merely says, "I wish Uncle Jack would allow him . . ." By substituting "that unfortunate young man, his brother," for "him," in preparing the 1899 edition, Wilde creates a new joke and an added layer to Cecily, whose parroting of Miss Prism's phrase has an ironic air about it.

Cecily. Dear Uncle Jack is so very serious! Sometimes he is so serious that I think he cannot be quite well.

Miss Prism. [*Drawing herself up.*] Your guardian enjoys the best of health, and his gravity of demeanour is especially to be commended in one so comparatively young as he is. I know no one who has a higher sense of duty and responsibility.

Cecily. I suppose that is why he often looks a little bored when we three are together.

Miss Prism. Cecily! I am surprised at you. Mr. Worthing has many troubles in his life. Idle merriment and triviality would be out of place in his conversation. You must remember his constant anxiety about that unfortunate young man his brother.

Cecily. I wish Uncle Jack would allow that unfortunate young man, his brother,[4] to come down here sometimes. We might have a good influence over him, Miss Prism. I am sure you certainly would. You know German, and geology, and things of that kind influence a man very much. [*Cecily begins to write in her diary.*]

Miss Prism. [*Shaking her head.*] I do not think that even I could produce any effect on a character that according to his own brother's admission is irretrievably weak and vacillating. Indeed I am not sure that I would desire to reclaim him. I am not in favour of this modern mania for

5. At a time when few publication venues were open to women, diaries and journals were an important medium for literate Victorian women. As Cecily implies, through the careful attention given to the minutiae of daily existence, the diarist gives meaning, form, and structure to an otherwise unnotable life. But diaries can also become a vehicle for constructing a private fantasy and an alternate self, and no less than memory, they can "chronicle the things that have never happened." Wilde wants us to question whether the secrets Cecily confides in her diary are as "wonderful" as she believes.

6. Mudie's Lending Library, with branches in London and other major English cities, was synonymous with the three-volume or "triple-decker" novels that it lent out to subscribers. Up until the mid-1890s, Victorian novels were, with rare exceptions, first published in a three-volume format, beyond the pockets of the vast majority of individual readers, leading to the growth of "Circulating" or "Lending" libraries such as Mudie's. For several decades, Mudie's had been one of the most powerful literary institutions in Victorian Britain, often acting as an unofficial censor by virtue of its great purchasing power. But by 1894, this power was on the wane, and by 1899, when *The Importance* was published, Mudie's was, like the three-volume novel itself, a spent force.

7. These lines of dialogue, containing Miss Prism's famous definition of fiction, from "Did you really, Miss Prism?" to "But it seems very unfair," were added in 1899.

turning bad people into good people at a moment's notice. As a man sows so let him reap. You must put away your diary, Cecily. I really don't see why you should keep a diary at all.

Cecily. I keep a diary in order to enter the wonderful secrets of my life.[5] If I didn't write them down, I should probably forget all about them.

Miss Prism. Memory, my dear Cecily, is the diary that we all carry about with us.

Cecily. Yes, but it usually chronicles the things that have never happened, and couldn't possibly have happened. I believe that Memory is responsible for nearly all the three-volume novels that Mudie sends us.[6]

Miss Prism. Do not speak slightingly of the three-volume novel, Cecily. I wrote one myself in earlier days.

Cecily. Did you really, Miss Prism? How wonderfully clever you are! I hope it did not end happily? I don't like novels that end happily. They depress me so much.[7]

Miss Prism. The good ended happily, and the bad unhappily. That is what Fiction means.

Cecily. I suppose so. But it seems very unfair. And was your novel ever published?

Miss Prism. Alas! no. The manuscript unfortunately was abandoned. [*Cecily starts.*] I use the word in the sense of lost

8. As opposed to dissolute or morally disreputable.

9. Cecily's fabrication of a headache, as the pretext for a tête-à-tête stroll, shows that she is not unaware of the unspoken sexual charge between Chasuble and Prism.

or mislaid.[8] To your work, child, these speculations are profitless.

Cecily. [*Smiling.*] But I see dear Dr. Chasuble coming up through the garden.

Miss Prism. [*Rising and advancing.*] Dr. Chasuble! This is indeed a pleasure.

[*Enter Canon Chasuble.*]

Chasuble. And how are we this morning? Miss Prism, you are, I trust, well?

Cecily. Miss Prism has just been complaining of a slight headache. I think it would do her so much good to have a short stroll with you in the Park, Dr. Chasuble.

Miss Prism. Cecily, I have not mentioned anything about a headache.[9]

Cecily. No, dear Miss Prism, I know that, but I felt instinctively that you had a headache. Indeed I was thinking about that, and not about my German lesson, when the Rector came in.

Chasuble. I hope, Cecily, you are not inattentive.

Cecily. Oh, I am afraid I am.

Chasuble. That is strange. Were I fortunate enough to be Miss Prism's pupil, I would hang upon her lips. [*Miss Prism glares.*] I spoke metaphorically.—My metaphor was drawn

10. Chasuble protests his sexual innocence, but Victorians were fascinated by bees' role in the sexual reproduction of plants, even though they often employed elaborate euphemisms and hasty evasions to suggest the contrary. In the writings of Wilde and his contemporaries, the bee is often a signifier for sexual activity, about which Victorians felt obliged to be circumspect.

11. According to the Roman historian Plutarch, Egeria was a nymph and minor goddess who imparted wisdom and prophecy in return for libations of water or milk at her sacred groves. She was counselor to the Roman king Numa Pompilius. As Chasuble's haste in describing it as "a classical allusion merely" indicates, his citation of Egeria and the "Pagan authors" highlights the superficiality of his Christian convictions.

12. The rupee, the currency of India, declined rapidly in value between 1873 and 1893.

13. Wilde substituted "sensational" for "exciting for a young girl" in 1899, while also adding, "Even these metallic problems have their melodramatic side."

from bees.[10] Ahem! Mr. Worthing, I suppose, has not returned from town yet?

Miss Prism. We do not expect him till Monday afternoon.

Chasuble. Ah yes, he usually likes to spend his Sunday in London. He is not one of those whose sole aim is enjoyment, as, by all accounts, that unfortunate young man his brother seems to be. But I must not disturb Egeria and her pupil any longer.

Miss Prism. Egeria? My name is Lætitia, Doctor.

Chasuble. [*Bowing.*] A classical allusion merely, drawn from the Pagan authors.[11] I shall see you both no doubt at Evensong?

Miss Prism. I think, dear Doctor, I will have a stroll with you. I find I have a headache after all, and a walk might do it good.

Chasuble. With pleasure, Miss Prism, with pleasure. We might go as far as the schools and back.

Miss Prism. That would be delightful. Cecily, you will read your Political Economy in my absence. The chapter on the Fall of the Rupee[12] you may omit. It is somewhat too sensational. Even these metallic problems have their melodramatic side.[13] [*Goes down the garden with Dr. Chasuble.*]

Cecily. [*Picks up books and throws them back on table.*] Horrid Political Economy! Horrid Geography! Horrid, horrid German!

14. Ernest Worthing's visiting card has mysteriously acquired a "W" (indicating that he resides in the district immediately west of London's center) since its introduction in Act 1. This appears to be an uncorrected error.

[*Enter Merriman with a card on a salver.*]

Merriman. Mr. Ernest Worthing has just driven over from the station. He has brought his luggage with him.

Cecily. [*Takes the card and reads it.*] "Mr. Ernest Worthing, B. 4, The Albany, W."[14] Uncle Jack's brother! Did you tell him Mr. Worthing was in town?

Merriman. Yes, Miss. He seemed very much disappointed. I mentioned that you and Miss Prism were in the garden. He said he was anxious to speak to you privately for a moment.

Cecily. Ask Mr. Ernest Worthing to come here. I suppose you had better talk to the housekeeper about a room for him.

Merriman. Yes, Miss. [*Merriman goes off.*]

Cecily. I have never met any really wicked person before. I feel rather frightened. I am so afraid he will look just like every one else.

[*Enter Algernon, very gay and debonnair.*]

He does!

Algernon. [*Raising his hat.*] You are my little cousin Cecily, I'm sure.

Cecily. You are under some strange mistake. I am not little. In fact, I believe I am more than usually tall for my age. [*Algernon is rather taken aback.*] But I am your cousin

15. This witty exchange, from Algernon's "I have a business appointment" to Cecily's "but still" three lines later, was added in 1899.

Cecily. You, I see from your card, are Uncle Jack's brother, my cousin Ernest, my wicked cousin Ernest.

Algernon. Oh! I am not really wicked at all, cousin Cecily. You mustn't think that I am wicked.

Cecily. If you are not, then you have certainly been deceiving us all in a very inexcusable manner. I hope you have not been leading a double life, pretending to be wicked and being really good all the time. That would be hypocrisy.

Algernon. [*Looks at her in amazement.*] Oh! Of course I have been rather reckless.

Cecily. I am glad to hear it.

Algernon. In fact, now you mention the subject, I have been very bad in my own small way.

Cecily. I don't think you should be so proud of that, though I am sure it must have been very pleasant.

Algernon. It is much pleasanter being here with you.

Cecily. I can't understand how you are here at all. Uncle Jack won't be back till Monday afternoon.

Algernon. That is a great disappointment. I am obliged to go up by the first train on Monday morning. I have a business appointment that I am anxious . . . to miss.[15]

Cecily. Couldn't you miss it anywhere but in London?

16. An early reviewer of Wilde's play disagreed, writing that "the effusive loveliness" of Jack's neckties "could scarcely fail to be attractive" (unsigned review of *The Importance of Being Earnest*, *Truth*, 21 Feb. 1895, repr. in *Oscar Wilde: The Critical Heritage*, ed. Karl Beckson [London: Routledge and Kegan Paul, 1970], 193).

Algernon. No: the appointment is in London.

Cecily. Well, I know, of course, how important it is not to keep a business engagement, if one wants to retain any sense of the beauty of life, but still I think you had better wait till Uncle Jack arrives. I know he wants to speak to you about your emigrating.

Algernon. About my what?

Cecily. Your emigrating. He has gone up to buy your outfit.

Algernon. I certainly wouldn't let Jack buy my outfit. He has no taste in neckties at all.[16]

Cecily. I don't think you will require neckties. Uncle Jack is sending you to Australia.

Algernon. Australia! I'd sooner die.

Cecily. Well, he said at dinner on Wednesday night, that you would have to choose between this world, the next world, and Australia.

Algernon. Oh, well! The accounts I have received of Australia and the next world, are not particularly encouraging. This world is good enough for me, cousin Cecily.

Cecily. Yes, but are you good enough for it?

Algernon. I'm afraid I'm not that. That is why I want you to reform me. You might make that your mission, if you don't mind, cousin Cecily.

17. A flower or floral decoration worn in the top button-hole. In "Phrases and Philosophies for the Use of the Young" (*The Chameleon*, December 1894), Wilde writes that "a really well-made button-hole is the only link between Art and Nature."

18. A species of yellow rose, cultivated in England from the 1860s onward, named for the French minister of war Marshal Adolphe Niel (1802–1869).

Cecily. I'm afraid I've no time, this afternoon.

Algernon. Well, would you mind my reforming myself this afternoon?

Cecily. It is rather Quixotic of you. But I think you should try.

Algernon. I will. I feel better already.

Cecily. You are looking a little worse.

Algernon. That is because I am hungry.

Cecily. How thoughtless of me. I should have remembered that when one is going to lead an entirely new life, one requires regular and wholesome meals. Won't you come in?

Algernon. Thank you. Might I have a button-hole first? I never have any appetite unless I have a button-hole[17] first.

Cecily. A Maréchal Niel?[18] [*Picks up scissors.*]

Algernon. No, I'd sooner have a pink rose.

Cecily. Why? [*Cuts a flower.*]

Algernon. Because you are like a pink rose, cousin Cecily.

Cecily. I don't think it can be right for you to talk to me like that. Miss Prism never says such things to me.

19. A *womanthrope,* coined from a humorous blend of "woman" and "misanthrope," is a hater of women or *misogynist.* Wilde had used the term earlier, in "The Critic as Artist," where he attributes it to "one of the pretty Newnham graduates" (*Criticism,* ed. Josephine M. Guy, vol. 4 of *The Complete Works of Oscar Wilde* [Oxford: Oxford University Press, 2007], 146). Although Canon Chasuble winces at "so neologistic a phrase," George Otto Trevelyan records encountering it "in a novel by a female hand" as early as 1863 (Trevelyan, "Letters of a Competition Wallah," *Macmillan's Magazine* 8 [July 1863]: 202–3).

Algernon. Then Miss Prism is a short-sighted old lady. [*Cecily puts the rose in his buttonhole.*] You are the prettiest girl I ever saw.

Cecily. Miss Prism says that all good looks are a snare.

Algernon. They are a snare that every sensible man would like to be caught in.

Cecily. Oh, I don't think I would care to catch a sensible man. I shouldn't know what to talk to him about.

[*They pass into the house. Miss Prism and Dr. Chasuble return.*]

Miss Prism. You are too much alone, dear Dr. Chasuble. You should get married. A misanthrope I can understand—a womanthrope, never![19]

Chasuble. [*With a scholar's shudder.*] Believe me, I do not deserve so neologistic a phrase. The precept as well as the practice of the Primitive Church was distinctly against matrimony.

Miss Prism. [*Sententiously.*] That is obviously the reason why the Primitive Church has not lasted up to the present day. And you do not seem to realise, dear Doctor, that by persistently remaining single, a man converts himself into a permanent public temptation. Men should be more careful; this very celibacy leads weaker vessels astray.

Chasuble. But is a man not equally attractive when married?

20. Though Miss Prism means *immature* or *undeveloped* and says she speaks horticulturally, Dr. Chasuble recoils at Miss Prism's implicit suggestion that young women are sexually innocent and easily gulled.

21. The brevity of the stage direction belies the fact that this is one of the funniest moments in the play. Early critics praised the subtle, hilarious effect produced by John Worthing's entrance in deep mourning (newly bereaved Victorians were expected to reflect their grief in a "garb of woe"), primed to announce the death of his brother Ernest, when the audience knows that "Ernest in the flesh—a false but undeniable Ernest—is at that moment in the house making love to Cecily. The audience does not instantly awaken to the meaning of his inky suit, but even as he marches solemnly down the stage, and before a word is spoken, you can feel the idea kindling from row to row, until a sudden glory of laughter fills the theatre" (William Àrcher, signed review of *The Importance of Being Earnest*, *World*, 20 Feb. 1895, repr. in Beckson, *Oscar Wilde*, 190).

Miss Prism. No married man is ever attractive except to his wife.

Chasuble. And often, I've been told, not even to her.

Miss Prism. That depends on the intellectual sympathies of the woman. Maturity can always be depended on. Ripeness can be trusted. Young women are green. [*Dr. Chasuble starts.*][20] I spoke horticulturally. My metaphor was drawn from fruits. But where is Cecily?

Chasuble. Perhaps she followed us to the schools.

[*Enter Jack slowly from the back of the garden. He is dressed in the deepest mourning, with crape hat-band and black gloves.*][21]

Miss Prism. Mr. Worthing!

Chasuble. Mr. Worthing?

Miss Prism. This is indeed a surprise. We did not look for you till Monday afternoon.

Jack. [*Shakes Miss Prism's hand in a tragic manner.*] I have returned sooner than I expected. Dr. Chasuble, I hope you are well?

Chasuble. Dear Mr. Worthing, I trust this garb of woe does not betoken some terrible calamity?

Jack. My brother.

22. A foreshadowing of Wilde's own death "abroad" in Paris, in the Hotel D'Alsace, in 1900, under the assumed name of "Sebastian Melmoth." Wilde had once written, "one should die as if one had never lived," and on his deathbed in 1900, he proclaimed, "I will never outlive this century, the English people would not stand for it" (quoted in Richard Ellmann, *Oscar Wilde* [New York: Knopf, 1988], 580).

23. Through the tedious repetition of Christ's words from Galatians 6:7, which she first quoted earlier in this scene, Miss Prism transforms a Christian proverb into a pedantic platitude.

Miss Prism. More shameful debts and extravagance?

Chasuble. Still leading his life of pleasure?

Jack. [*Shaking his head.*] Dead!

Chasuble. Your brother Ernest dead?

Jack. Quite dead.

Miss Prism. What a lesson for him! I trust he will profit by it.

Chasuble. Mr. Worthing, I offer you my sincere condolence. You have at least the consolation of knowing that you were always the most generous and forgiving of brothers.

Jack. Poor Ernest! He had many faults, but it is a sad, sad blow.

Chasuble. Very sad indeed. Were you with him at the end?

Jack. No. He died abroad; in Paris, in fact. I had a telegram last night from the manager of the Grand Hotel.[22]

Chasuble. Was the cause of death mentioned?

Jack. A severe chill, it seems.

Miss Prism. As a man sows, so shall he reap.[23]

Chasuble. [*Raising his hand.*] Charity, dear Miss Prism, charity! None of us are perfect. I myself am peculiarly susceptible to draughts. Will the interment take place here?

24. Another witticism sharpened and made politically pointed for the first edition of 1899. The entirely fictive "Society for the Prevention of Discontent among the Upper Orders" was originally the real-life "Society for the Prevention of Cruelty to Children." Wilde initially altered this to "Society for the Prevention of Discontent among the Lower Orders" in preparing the 1899 edition, before changing "Lower Orders" to "Upper Orders" in proof.

Jack. No. He seems to have expressed a desire to be buried in Paris.

Chasuble. In Paris! [*Shakes his head.*] I fear that hardly points to any very serious state of mind at the last. You would no doubt wish me to make some slight allusion to this tragic domestic affliction next Sunday. [*Jack presses his hand convulsively.*] My sermon on the meaning of the manna in the wilderness can be adapted to almost any occasion, joyful, or, as in the present case, distressing. [*All sigh.*] I have preached it at harvest celebrations, christenings, confirmations, on days of humiliation and festal days. The last time I delivered it was in the Cathedral, as a charity sermon on behalf of the Society for the Prevention of Discontent among the Upper Orders.[24] The Bishop, who was present, was much struck by some of the analogies I drew.

Jack. Ah! that reminds me, you mentioned christenings I think, Dr. Chasuble? I suppose you know how to christen all right? [*Dr. Chasuble looks astounded.*] I mean, of course, you are continually christening, aren't you?

Miss Prism. It is, I regret to say, one of the Rector's most constant duties in this parish. I have often spoken to the poorer classes on the subject. But they don't seem to know what thrift is.

Chasuble. But is there any particular infant in whom you are interested, Mr. Worthing? Your brother was, I believe, unmarried, was he not?

CECILY CARDEW, WORTHING'S WARD (MISS MILLARD).

" I keep a diary in order to enter the wonderful secrets of my life. If I didn't write them down, I would probably forget all about them."

"I keep a diary to enter the wonderful secrets of my life," publicity still from *The Sketch*, March 20, 1895. Widener Library, Harvard University.

Jack. Oh yes.

Miss Prism. [*Bitterly.*] People who live entirely for pleasure usually are.

Jack. But it is not for any child, dear Doctor. I am very fond of children. No! the fact is, I would like to be christened myself, this afternoon, if you have nothing better to do.

Chasuble. But surely, Mr. Worthing, you have been christened already?

Jack. I don't remember anything about it.

Chasuble. But have you any grave doubts on the subject?

Jack. I certainly intend to have. Of course I don't know if the thing would bother you in any way, or if you think I am a little too old now.

Chasuble. Not at all. The sprinkling, and, indeed, the immersion of adults is a perfectly canonical practice.

Jack. Immersion!

Chasuble. You need have no apprehensions. Sprinkling is all that is necessary, or indeed I think advisable. Our weather is so changeable. At what hour would you wish the ceremony performed?

Jack. Oh, I might trot round about five if that would suit you.

JOHN WORTHING, J.P. (MR. GEORGE ALEXANDER).

"*My poor brother Ernest!*"

"Poor Ernest!" publicity still from *The Sketch*, March 20, 1895. Widener Library, Harvard University.

Chasuble. Perfectly, perfectly! In fact I have two similar ceremonies to perform at that time. A case of twins that occurred recently in one of the outlying cottages on your own estate. Poor Jenkins the carter, a most hard-working man.

Jack. Oh! I don't see much fun in being christened along with other babies. It would be childish. Would half-past five do?

Chasuble. Admirably! Admirably! [*Takes out watch.*] And now, dear Mr. Worthing, I will not intrude any longer into a house of sorrow. I would merely beg you not to be too much bowed down by grief. What seem to us bitter trials are often blessings in disguise.

Miss Prism. This seems to me a blessing of an extremely obvious kind.

[*Enter Cecily from the house.*]

Cecily. Uncle Jack! Oh, I am pleased to see you back. But what horrid clothes you have got on! Do go and change them.

Miss Prism. Cecily!

Chasuble. My child! my child! [*Cecily goes towards Jack; he kisses her brow in a melancholy manner.*]

Cecily. What is the matter, Uncle Jack? Do look happy! You look as if you had toothache, and I have got such a surprise

25. "Oh, brothers!," declares Lord Henry Wotton in *The Picture of Dorian Gray*. "I don't care for brothers. My elder brother won't die, and my younger brothers seem never to do anything else. . . . I can't help detesting my relations. I suppose it comes from the fact that we can't stand other people having the same faults as ourselves" (*The Picture of Dorian Gray: An Annotated, Uncensored Edition*, pp. 82–83).

for you. Who do you think is in the dining-room? Your brother!

Jack. Who?

Cecily. Your brother Ernest. He arrived about half an hour ago.

Jack. What nonsense! I haven't got a brother.

Cecily. Oh, don't say that. However badly he may have behaved to you in the past he is still your brother. You couldn't be so heartless as to disown him.[25] I'll tell him to come out. And you will shake hands with him, won't you, Uncle Jack? [*Runs back into the house.*]

Chasuble. These are very joyful tidings.

Miss Prism. After we had all been resigned to his loss, his sudden return seems to me peculiarly distressing.

Jack. My brother is in the dining-room? I don't know what it all means. I think it is perfectly absurd.

[*Enter Algernon and Cecily hand in hand. They come slowly up to Jack.*]

Jack. Good heavens! [*Motions Algernon away.*]

Algernon. Brother John, I have come down from town to tell you that I am very sorry for all the trouble I have given you, and that I intend to lead a better life in the future. [*Jack glares at him and does not take his hand.*]

26. Wilde only introduced much of this comical exchange in 1899, deliberately playing off Cecily's pathos against Jack's intemperate replies.

Cecily. Uncle Jack, you are not going to refuse your own brother's hand?

Jack. Nothing will induce me to take his hand. I think his coming down here disgraceful. He knows perfectly well why.

Cecily. Uncle Jack, do be nice. There is some good in every one. Ernest has just been telling me about his poor invalid friend Mr. Bunbury whom he goes to visit so often. And surely there must be much good in one who is kind to an invalid, and leaves the pleasures of London to sit by a bed of pain.[26]

Jack. Oh! he has been talking about Bunbury, has he?

Cecily. Yes, he has told me all about poor Mr. Bunbury, and his terrible state of health.

Jack. Bunbury! Well, I won't have him talk to you about Bunbury or about anything else. It is enough to drive one perfectly frantic.

Algernon. Of course I admit that the faults were all on my side. But I must say that I think that Brother John's coldness to me is peculiarly painful. I expected a more enthusiastic welcome, especially considering it is the first time I have come here.

Cecily. Uncle Jack, if you don't shake hands with Ernest I will never forgive you.

Leaf from Wilde's holograph draft, c. September 1894, showing the opening of Act 3 (later renumbered Act 2). The play was originally written in four acts, and Wilde used a false title to keep the play's real title a strict secret. "It is called *Lady Lancing* on the cover," Wilde explained to the actor-manager George Alexander, "but the real title is *The Importance of Being Earnest*." © The Estate of Oscar Wilde/The British Library Board, ADD. 37948.f14.

Jack. Never forgive me?

Cecily. Never, never, never!

Jack. Well, this is the last time I shall ever do it. [*Shakes hands with Algernon and glares.*]

Chasuble. It's pleasant, is it not, to see so perfect a reconciliation? I think we might leave the two brothers together.

Miss Prism. Cecily, you will come with us.

Cecily. Certainly, Miss Prism. My little task of reconciliation is over.

Chasuble. You have done a beautiful action to-day, dear child.

Miss Prism. We must not be premature in our judgments.

Cecily. I feel very happy. [*They all go off except Jack and Algernon.*]

Jack. You young scoundrel, Algy, you must get out of this place as soon as possible. I don't allow any Bunburying here.

[*Enter Merriman.*]

Merriman. I have put Mr. Ernest's things in the room next to yours, sir. I suppose that is all right?

Jack. What?

27. These telling details about Algernon's luggage, all expressive of Algernon's self-indulgence, were added in 1899.

28. A light horse-drawn cart, once popular with hunters but widely fashionable in the 1890s, with two transverse seats back to back, the rear seat originally converting into a box for dogs.

29. In reducing the play from four to three acts, Wilde eliminated a scene at this juncture in which a solicitor named Gribsby arrives and serves a writ of attachment on Algernon (in the character of Ernest) for debts accumulated at the Savoy Hotel. For the original scene, see *The Definitive Four-Act Version of The Importance of Being Earnest*, ed. Ruth Berggren (New York: Vanguard, 1987), 118–25.

30. This witticism and much of the intemperate exchange between Jack and Algernon, from "What a fearful liar" to "I can quite understand that," were added in 1899.

Merriman. Mr. Ernest's luggage, sir. I have unpacked it and put it in the room next to your own.

Jack. His luggage?

Merriman. Yes, sir. Three portmanteaus, a dressing-case, two hat-boxes, and a large luncheon-basket.[27]

Algernon. I am afraid I can't stay more than a week this time.

Jack. Merriman, order the dog-cart[28] at once. Mr. Ernest has been suddenly called back to town.

Merriman. Yes, sir. [*Goes back into the house.*][29]

Algernon. What a fearful liar you are, Jack. I have not been called back to town at all.

Jack. Yes, you have.

Algernon. I haven't heard any one call me.

Jack. Your duty as a gentleman calls you back.

Algernon. My duty as a gentleman has never interfered with my pleasures in the smallest degree.[30]

Jack. I can quite understand that.

Algernon. Well, Cecily is a darling.

Jack. You are not to talk of Miss Cardew like that. I don't like it.

31. This famous and witty line of dialogue, based on one of Wilde's "Phrases and Philosophies for the Use of the Young" (*Chameleon*, December 1894), was inserted in 1899, along with Jack's reply ("Your vanity is ridiculous. . . . This Bunburying, as you call it, has not been a great success for you") and Algernon's subsequent assertion, "I think it has been a great success."

Algernon. Well, I don't like your clothes. You look perfectly ridiculous in them. Why on earth don't you go up and change? It is perfectly childish to be in deep mourning for a man who is actually staying for a whole week with you in your house as a guest. I call it grotesque.

Jack. You are certainly not staying with me for a whole week as a guest or anything else. You have got to leave . . . by the four-five train.

Algernon. I certainly won't leave you so long as you are in mourning. It would be most unfriendly. If I were in mourning you would stay with me, I suppose. I should think it very unkind if you didn't.

Jack. Well, will you go if I change my clothes?

Algernon. Yes, if you are not too long. I never saw anybody take so long to dress, and with such little result.

Jack. Well, at any rate, that is better than being always over-dressed as you are.

Algernon. If I am occasionally a little over-dressed, I make up for it by being always immensely over-educated.[31]

Jack. Your vanity is ridiculous, your conduct an outrage, and your presence in my garden utterly absurd. However, you have got to catch the four-five, and I hope you will have a pleasant journey back to town. This Bunburying, as you call it, has not been a great success for you. [*Goes into the house.*]

32. "and make arrangements for another Bunbury" was added in 1899.

Algernon. I think it has been a great success. I'm in love with Cecily, and that is everything.

[*Enter Cecily at the back of the garden. She picks up the can and begins to water the flowers.*]

But I must see her before I go, and make arrangements for another Bunbury.[32] Ah, there she is.

Cecily. Oh, I merely came back to water the roses. I thought you were with Uncle Jack.

Algernon. He's gone to order the dog-cart for me.

Cecily. Oh, is he going to take you for a nice drive?

Algernon. He's going to send me away.

Cecily. Then have we got to part?

Algernon. I am afraid so. It's a very painful parting.

Cecily. It is always painful to part from people whom one has known for a very brief space of time. The absence of old friends one can endure with equanimity. But even a momentary separation from anyone to whom one has just been introduced is almost unbearable.

Algernon. Thank you.

[*Enter Merriman.*]

Merriman. The dog-cart is at the door, sir. [*Algernon looks appealingly at Cecily.*]

33. Cecily, by declaring her diary "meant for publication," articulates an unspoken wish motivating many diarists. While the diary is an intensely private form of writing, the diarist often secretly imagines an audience different and potentially wider than the self who writes. By adding "When it appears in volume form I hope you will order a copy," in 1899, Wilde acknowledges the growing number of diaries by women published in his own day (Queen Victoria, Fanny Burney, Dorothy Wordsworth) and anticipates those by important modern women (Edith Wharton, Virginia Woolf, Katherine Mansfield, Anne Frank) that were published in the next few decades.

Cecily. It can wait, Merriman . . . for . . . five minutes.

Merriman. Yes, Miss. [*Exit Merriman.*]

Algernon. I hope, Cecily, I shall not offend you if I state quite frankly and openly that you seem to me to be in every way the visible personification of absolute perfection.

Cecily. I think your frankness does you great credit, Ernest. If you will allow me, I will copy your remarks into my diary. [*Goes over to table and begins writing in diary.*]

Algernon. Do you really keep a diary? I'd give anything to look at it. May I?

Cecily. Oh no. [*Puts her hand over it.*] You see, it is simply a very young girl's record of her own thoughts and impressions, and consequently meant for publication.[33] When it appears in volume form I hope you will order a copy. But pray, Ernest, don't stop. I delight in taking down from dictation. I have reached "absolute perfection." You can go on. I am quite ready for more.

Algernon. [*Somewhat taken aback.*] Ahem! Ahem!

Cecily. Oh, don't cough, Ernest. When one is dictating one should speak fluently and not cough. Besides, I don't know how to spell a cough. [*Writes as Algernon speaks.*]

Algernon. [*Speaking very rapidly.*] Cecily, ever since I first looked upon your wonderful and incomparable beauty,

34. This line of dialogue and the two following it represent Wilde's condensation of a longer scene, in his original four-act drafts, in which Cecily painstakingly transcribes Algernon's professions of love into her diary. For the original scene, see *The Definitive Four-Act Version of The Importance of Being Earnest*, ed. Berggren, 136–38.

I have dared to love you wildly, passionately, devotedly, hopelessly.[34]

Cecily. I don't think that you should tell me that you love me wildly, passionately, devotedly, hopelessly. Hopelessly doesn't seem to make much sense, does it?

Algernon. Cecily!

[*Enter Merriman.*]

Merriman. The dog-cart is waiting, sir.

Algernon. Tell it to come round next week, at the same hour.

Merriman. [*Looks at Cecily, who makes no sign.*] Yes, sir.

[*Merriman retires.*]

Cecily. Uncle Jack would be very much annoyed if he knew you were staying on till next week, at the same hour.

Algernon. Oh, I don't care about Jack. I don't care for anybody in the whole world but you. I love you, Cecily. You will marry me, won't you?

Cecily. You silly boy! Of course. Why, we have been engaged for the last three months.

Algernon. For the last three months?

Cecily. Yes, it will be exactly three months on Thursday.

Algernon. But how did we become engaged?

Cecily. Well, ever since dear Uncle Jack first confessed to us that he had a younger brother who was very wicked and bad, you of course have formed the chief topic of conversation between myself and Miss Prism. And of course a man who is much talked about is always very attractive. One feels there must be something in him, after all. I daresay it was foolish of me, but I fell in love with you, Ernest.

Algernon. Darling! And when was the engagement actually settled?

Cecily. On the 14th of February last. Worn out by your entire ignorance of my existence, I determined to end the matter one way or the other, and after a long struggle with myself I accepted you under this dear old tree here. The next day I bought this little ring in your name, and this is the little bangle with the true lovers' knot I promised you always to wear.

Algernon. Did I give you this? It's very pretty, isn't it?

Cecily. Yes, you've wonderfully good taste, Ernest. It's the excuse I've always given for your leading such a bad life. And this is the box in which I keep all your dear letters. [*Kneels at table, opens box, and produces letters tied up with blue ribbon.*]

Algernon. My letters! But, my own sweet Cecily, I have never written you any letters.

35. Although the diarist purportedly chronicles reality, frequently she constructs an alternate reality: as Judy Simons observes, "the more we read others' diaries, the more we become aware of the diary's fictive quality, and of the creation of a central character, established through an act of imagination as powerful as those for stimulating writers' published works" (Simons, *Diaries and Journals of Literary Women, from Fanny Burney to Virginia Woolf* [Iowa City: University of Iowa Press, 1990], 196).

Cecily. You need hardly remind me of that, Ernest. I remember only too well that I was forced to write your letters for you. I wrote always three times a week, and sometimes oftener.

Algernon. Oh, do let me read them, Cecily?

Cecily. Oh, I couldn't possibly. They would make you far too conceited. [*Replaces box.*] The three you wrote me after I had broken off the engagement are so beautiful, and so badly spelled, that even now I can hardly read them without crying a little.

Algernon. But was our engagement ever broken off?

Cecily. Of course it was. On the 22nd of last March. You can see the entry if you like. [*Shows diary.*] "To-day I broke off my engagement with Ernest. I feel it is better to do so. The weather still continues charming."[35]

Algernon. But why on earth did you break it off? What had I done? I had done nothing at all. Cecily, I am very much hurt indeed to hear you broke it off. Particularly when the weather was so charming.

Cecily. It would hardly have been a really serious engagement if it hadn't been broken off at least once. But I forgave you before the week was out.

Algernon. [*Crossing to her, and kneeling.*] What a perfect angel you are, Cecily.

CECILY AND MONCRIEFFE.

CECILY : " *I hope your hair curls naturally.*"
MONCRIEFFE : " *Yes, darling, with a little help from others.*"

"I hope your hair curls naturally," publicity still from *The Sketch,*
March 20, 1895. Widener Library, Harvard University.

Cecily. You dear romantic boy. [*He kisses her, she puts her fingers through his hair.*] I hope your hair curls naturally, does it?

Algernon. Yes, darling, with a little help from others.

Cecily. I am so glad.

Algernon. You'll never break off our engagement again, Cecily?

Cecily. I don't think I could break it off now that I have actually met you. Besides, of course, there is the question of your name.

Algernon. Yes, of course. [*Nervously.*]

Cecily. You must not laugh at me, darling, but it had always been a girlish dream of mine to love some one whose name was Ernest. [*Algernon rises, Cecily also.*] There is something in that name that seems to inspire absolute confidence. I pity any poor married woman whose husband is not called Ernest.

Algernon. But, my dear child, do you mean to say you could not love me if I had some other name?

Cecily. But what name?

Algernon. Oh, any name you like—Algernon—for instance . . .

Cecily. But I don't like the name of Algernon.

36. "Half of the chaps who get into the Bankruptcy Court are called Algernon" was added in 1899.

Algernon. Well, my own dear, sweet, loving little darling, I really can't see why you should object to the name of Algernon. It is not at all a bad name. In fact, it is rather an aristocratic name. Half of the chaps who get into the Bankruptcy Court are called Algernon.[36] But seriously, Cecily . . . [*Moving to her*] . . . if my name was Algy, couldn't you love me?

Cecily. [*Rising.*] I might respect you, Ernest, I might admire your character, but I fear that I should not be able to give you my undivided attention.

Algernon. Ahem! Cecily! [*Picking up hat.*] Your Rector here is, I suppose, thoroughly experienced in the practice of all the rites and ceremonials of the Church?

Cecily. Oh, yes. Dr. Chasuble is a most learned man. He has never written a single book, so you can imagine how much he knows.

Algernon. I must see him at once on a most important christening—I mean on most important business.

Cecily. Oh!

Algernon. I shan't be away more than half an hour.

Cecily. Considering that we have been engaged since February the 14th, and that I only met you to-day for the first time, I think it is rather hard that you should leave me for so long a period as half an hour. Couldn't you make it twenty minutes?

37. Cecily's dislike of women who perform philanthropic work is foreshadowed in *The Picture of Dorian Gray* by Lord Henry Wotton's distaste for his Aunt Agatha, who, he relates, "told me she had discovered a wonderful young man, who was going to help her in the East End" (*The Picture of Dorian Gray: An Annotated, Uncensored Edition*, 87). In Wilde's day, well-to-do women assumed a central role as social activists in working-class districts such as London's East End. The English historian Jane Lewis writes that "taking a district" was "something that large numbers of young middle-class women felt obliged to do before marriage, and many carried on the work throughout their adult lives" (*Women and Social Action in Victorian and Edwardian England* [Stanford U. P., 1991], p. 10). According to Lewis, such work "remained within the bounds of propriety and middle-class women's sphere" while answering a need to serve others that was widely perceived to constitute women's main obligation as active citizens (p. 11).

Algernon. I'll be back in no time. [*Kisses her and rushes down the garden.*]

Cecily. What an impetuous boy he is! I like his hair so much. I must enter his proposal in my diary.

[*Enter Merriman.*]

Merriman. A Miss Fairfax has just called to see Mr. Worthing. On very important business, Miss Fairfax states.

Cecily. Isn't Mr. Worthing in his library?

Merriman. Mr. Worthing went over in the direction of the Rectory some time ago.

Cecily. Pray ask the lady to come out here; Mr. Worthing is sure to be back soon. And you can bring tea.

Merriman. Yes, Miss. [*Goes out.*]

Cecily. Miss Fairfax! I suppose one of the many good elderly women who are associated with Uncle Jack in some of his philanthropic work in London. I don't quite like women who are interested in philanthropic work.[37] I think it is so forward of them.

[*Enter Merriman.*]

Merriman. Miss Fairfax.

[*Enter Gwendolen.*] [*Exit Merriman.*]

Cecily. [*Advancing to meet her.*] Pray let me introduce myself to you. My name is Cecily Cardew.

Gwendolen. Cecily Cardew? [*Moving to her and shaking hands.*] What a very sweet name! Something tells me that we are going to be great friends. I like you already more than I can say. My first impressions of people are never wrong.

Cecily. How nice of you to like me so much after we have known each other such a comparatively short time. Pray sit down.

Gwendolen. [*Still standing up.*] I may call you Cecily, may I not?

Cecily. With pleasure!

Gwendolen. And you will always call me Gwendolen, won't you?

Cecily. If you wish.

Gwendolen. Then that is all quite settled, is it not?

Cecily. I hope so. [*A pause. They both sit down together.*]

Gwendolen. Perhaps this might be a favourable opportunity for my mentioning who I am. My father is Lord Bracknell. You have never heard of papa, I suppose?

Cecily. I don't think so.

38. "it is part of her system" was added in 1899.

39. "A pair of eye-glasses held in the hand, usually by a long metal, ivory, or tortoise-shell handle" (*Oxford English Dictionary*, s.v. "lorgnette"), a necessary prop for several of Wilde's female characters, whom Wilde suggests have poorer vision than their male counterparts do. Mrs. Allonby in *A Woman of No Importance* and Lady Basildon in *An Ideal Husband* also employ a lorgnette, while in the first production of *The Importance of Being Earnest*, Lady Bracknell brandished a lorgnette "suspended from a short gilt chain with pearl links" (review in *Illustrated Sporting and Dramatic News*, 30 Mar. 1895, quoted in editorial note to *Oscar Wilde's "The Importance of Being Earnest": A Reconstructive Critical Edition*, ed. Joseph Donohue, with Ruth Berggren [Gerrards Cross, UK: Colin Smythe, 1995], 136). In 1887, Wilde briefly reviewed plays for the *Court and Society Review* under the pseudonym "The Lorgnette."

Gwendolen. Outside the family circle, papa, I am glad to say, is entirely unknown. I think that is quite as it should be. The home seems to me to be the proper sphere for the man. And certainly once a man begins to neglect his domestic duties he becomes painfully effeminate, does he not? And I don't like that. It makes men so very attractive. Cecily, mamma, whose views on education are remarkably strict, has brought me up to be extremely short-sighted; it is part of her system;[38] so do you mind my looking at you through my glasses?

Cecily. Oh! not at all, Gwendolen. I am very fond of being looked at.

Gwendolen. [*After examining Cecily carefully through a lorgnette.*[39]] You are here on a short visit, I suppose.

Cecily. Oh no! I live here.

Gwendolen. [*Severely.*] Really? Your mother, no doubt, or some female relative of advanced years, resides here also?

Cecily. Oh no! I have no mother, nor, in fact, any relations.

Gwendolen. Indeed?

Cecily. My dear guardian, with the assistance of Miss Prism, has the arduous task of looking after me.

Gwendolen. Your guardian?

40. This ironical sentence was added in 1899.

41. This sentence and the next, from "Modern" to "unreadable," were added in 1899.

Cecily. Yes, I am Mr. Worthing's ward.

Gwendolen. Oh! It is strange he never mentioned to me that he had a ward. How secretive of him! He grows more interesting hourly. I am not sure, however, that the news inspires me with feelings of unmixed delight. [*Rising and going to her.*] I am very fond of you, Cecily; I have liked you ever since I met you! But I am bound to state that now that I know that you are Mr. Worthing's ward, I cannot help expressing a wish you were—well, just a little older than you seem to be—and not quite so very alluring in appearance. In fact, if I may speak candidly—

Cecily. Pray do! I think that whenever one has anything unpleasant to say, one should always be quite candid.

Gwendolen. Well, to speak with perfect candour, Cecily, I wish that you were fully forty-two, and more than usually plain for your age. Ernest has a strong upright nature. He is the very soul of truth and honour. Disloyalty would be as impossible to him as deception.[40] But even men of the noblest possible moral character are extremely susceptible to the influence of the physical charms of others. Modern, no less than Ancient History, supplies us with many most painful examples of what I refer to.[41] If it were not so, indeed, History would be quite unreadable.

Cecily. I beg your pardon, Gwendolen, did you say Ernest?

Gwendolen. Yes.

Cecily. Oh, but it is not Mr. Ernest Worthing who is my guardian. It is his brother—his elder brother.

Gwendolen. [*Sitting down again.*] Ernest never mentioned to me that he had a brother.

Cecily. I am sorry to say they have not been on good terms for a long time.

Gwendolen. Ah! that accounts for it. And now that I think of it I have never heard any man mention his brother. The subject seems distasteful to most men. Cecily, you have lifted a load from my mind. I was growing almost anxious. It would have been terrible if any cloud had come across a friendship like ours, would it not? Of course you are quite, quite sure that it is not Mr. Ernest Worthing who is your guardian?

Cecily. Quite sure. [*A pause.*] In fact, I am going to be his.

Gwendolen. [*Enquiringly.*] I beg your pardon?

Cecily. [*Rather shy and confidingly.*] Dearest Gwendolen, there is no reason why I should make a secret of it to you. Our little county newspaper is sure to chronicle the fact next week. Mr. Ernest Worthing and I are engaged to be married.

Gwendolen. [*Quite politely, rising.*] My darling Cecily, I think there must be some slight error. Mr. Ernest Worthing

42. Prominent conservative London daily newspaper, noted for its attention to the activities of the powerful and the wealthy. With a substantial readership among London's elite, it contrasts markedly with the "little county newspaper" that Cecily expects to chronicle her engagement to Ernest/Algernon. As Joseph Donohue observes (editorial note, *Oscar Wilde's "The Importance of Being Earnest": A Reconstructive Critical Edition*, 271), in an early draft Lady Bracknell (named "Lady Brancaster" in early drafts) calls the *Morning Post* "the only document of our time from which the history of the English people in the XIXth century could be written with any regard to decorum or even decency."

is engaged to me. The announcement will appear in the *Morning Post*[42] on Saturday at the latest.

Cecily. [*Very politely, rising.*] I am afraid you must be under some misconception. Ernest proposed to me exactly ten minutes ago. [*Shows diary.*]

Gwendolen. [*Examines diary through her lorgnette carefully.*] It is certainly very curious, for he asked me to be his wife yesterday afternoon at 5.30. If you would care to verify the incident, pray do so. [*Produces diary of her own.*] I never travel without my diary. One should always have something sensational to read in the train. I am so sorry, dear Cecily, if it is any disappointment to you, but I am afraid I have the prior claim.

Cecily. It would distress me more than I can tell you, dear Gwendolen, if it caused you any mental or physical anguish, but I feel bound to point out that since Ernest proposed to you he clearly has changed his mind.

Gwendolen. [*Meditatively.*] If the poor fellow has been entrapped into any foolish promise I shall consider it my duty to rescue him at once, and with a firm hand.

Cecily. [*Thoughtfully and sadly.*] Whatever unfortunate entanglement my dear boy may have got into, I will never reproach him with it after we are married.

Gwendolen. Do you allude to me, Miss Cardew, as an entanglement? You are presumptuous. On an occasion of

43. "I would like to protest against the statement that I have ever called a spade a spade," Wilde once remarked. "The man who did so should be condemned to use one" (quoted in Ellmann, *Oscar Wilde*, p. 368). A similar version of Wilde's quip appears in the 1891 version of *The Picture of Dorian Gray.*

this kind it becomes more than a moral duty to speak one's mind. It becomes a pleasure.

Cecily. Do you suggest, Miss Fairfax, that I entrapped Ernest into an engagement? How dare you? This is no time for wearing the shallow mask of manners. When I see a spade I call it a spade.[43]

Gwendolen. [*Satirically.*] I am glad to say that I have never seen a spade. It is obvious that our social spheres have been widely different.

[*Enter Merriman, followed by the footman. He carries a salver, table cloth, and plate stand. Cecily is about to retort. The presence of the servants exercises a restraining influence, under which both girls chafe.*]

Merriman. Shall I lay tea here as usual, Miss?

Cecily. [*Sternly, in a calm voice.*] Yes, as usual. [*Merriman begins to clear table and lay cloth. A long pause. Cecily and Gwendolen glare at each other.*]

Gwendolen. Are there many interesting walks in the vicinity, Miss Cardew?

Cecily. Oh! yes! a great many. From the top of one of the hills quite close one can see five counties.

Gwendolen. Five counties! I don't think I should like that; I hate crowds.

44. Cecily puns on *common*, as meaning both "commonplace" and "of low rank" or undistinguished, to make her riposte more barbed.

45. "Everywhere we are hearing of agricultural depression," remarked the *Contemporary Review* in November 1893 (vol. 64, p. 640): "everybody is deploring the exodus of our populations from the rural districts, and the desperate and fatal increase of population in each of our towns." This depression had been under way since the late 1870s, driven partly by a steep decline in the price of wheat and other cereals (see Richard Perren, *Agriculture in Depression, 1870–1940* [Cambridge: Cambridge University Press, 1995], 7–16), and in 1893, a Royal Commission was appointed to inquire into it. As Lady Bracknell's remark in Act 1 that "land has ceased to be either a profit or a pleasure" implies, agricultural depression had by 1895 affected the aristocratic or landed class markedly. The historian David Cannadine observes, "The world-wide collapse in agricultural prices meant that estate rentals fell dramatically, and that land values plummeted accordingly. As a result, the whole territorial basis of patrician existence was undermined" (Cannadine, *The Decline and Fall of the British Aristocracy* [1990; repr., New York: Vintage, 1999], 27).

Cecily. [*Sweetly.*] I suppose that is why you live in town?
[*Gwendolen bites her lip, and beats her foot nervously with
her parasol.*]

Gwendolen. [*Looking round.*] Quite a well-kept garden this
is, Miss Cardew.

Cecily. So glad you like it, Miss Fairfax.

Gwendolen. I had no idea there were any flowers in the
country.

Cecily. Oh, flowers are as common here, Miss Fairfax, as
people are in London.[44]

Gwendolen. Personally I cannot understand how anybody
manages to exist in the country, if anybody who is anybody
does. The country always bores me to death.

Cecily. Ah! This is what the newspapers call agricultural
depression, is it not? I believe the aristocracy are suffering
very much from it just at present.[45] It is almost an epidemic
amongst them, I have been told. May I offer you some tea,
Miss Fairfax?

Gwendolen. [*With elaborate politeness.*] Thank you. [*Aside.*]
Detestable girl! But I require tea!

Cecily. [*Sweetly.*] Sugar?

Gwendolen. [*Superciliously.*] No, thank you. Sugar is not
fashionable any more. [*Cecily looks angrily at her, takes up
the tongs and puts four lumps of sugar into the cup.*]

46. The bitterest interpersonal disagreements, in *The Importance of Being Earnest*, are displaced onto food: Cecily's aggression with sugar and tea cake echoes Algernon's truculence about cucumber sandwiches, in Act 1, as well as his quarrel with Jack over muffins at the end of the present act.

Cecily. [*Severely.*] Cake or bread and butter?

Gwendolen. [*In a bored manner.*] Bread and butter, please. Cake is rarely seen at the best houses nowadays.

Cecily. [*Cuts a very large slice of cake, and puts it on the tray.*] Hand that to Miss Fairfax.

[*Merriman does so, and goes out with footman. Gwendolen drinks the tea and makes a grimace. Puts down cup at once, reaches out her hand to the bread and butter, looks at it, and finds it is cake. Rises in indignation.*]

Gwendolen. You have filled my tea with lumps of sugar, and though I asked most distinctly for bread and butter, you have given me cake.[46] I am known for the gentleness of my disposition, and the extraordinary sweetness of my nature, but I warn you, Miss Cardew, you may go too far.

Cecily. [*Rising.*] To save my poor, innocent, trusting boy from the machinations of any other girl there are no lengths to which I would not go.

Gwendolen. From the moment I saw you I distrusted you. I felt that you were false and deceitful. I am never deceived in such matters. My first impressions of people are invariably right.

Cecily. It seems to me, Miss Fairfax, that I am trespassing on your valuable time. No doubt you have many other calls of a similar character to make in the neighbourhood.

[*Enter Jack.*]

Gwendolen. [*Catching sight of him.*] Ernest! My own
Ernest!

Jack. Gwendolen! Darling! [*Offers to kiss her.*]

Gwendolen. [*Draws back.*] A moment! May I ask if you
are engaged to be married to this young lady? [*Points to
Cecily.*]

Jack. [*Laughing.*] To dear little Cecily! Of course not!
What could have put such an idea into your pretty little
head?

Gwendolen. Thank you. You may! [*Offers her cheek.*]

Cecily. [*Very sweetly.*] I knew there must be some misunderstanding, Miss Fairfax. The gentleman whose arm is at
present round your waist is my guardian, Mr. John
Worthing.

Gwendolen. I beg your pardon?

Cecily. This is Uncle Jack.

Gwendolen. [*Receding.*] Jack! Oh!

[*Enter Algernon.*]

Cecily. Here is Ernest.

Algernon. [*Goes straight over to Cecily without noticing any
one else.*] My own love! [*Offers to kiss her.*]

Cecily. [*Drawing back.*] A moment, Ernest! May I ask you—are you engaged to be married to this young lady?

Algernon. [*Looking round.*] To what young lady? Good heavens! Gwendolen!

Cecily. Yes! to good heavens, Gwendolen, I mean to Gwendolen.

Algernon. [*Laughing.*] Of course not! What could have put such an idea into your pretty little head?

Cecily. Thank you. [*Presenting her cheek to be kissed.*] You may. [*Algernon kisses her.*]

Gwendolen. I felt there was some slight error, Miss Cardew. The gentleman who is now embracing you is my cousin, Mr. Algernon Moncrieff.

Cecily. [*Breaking away from Algernon.*] Algernon Moncrieff! Oh! [*The two girls move towards each other and put their arms round each other's waists as if for protection.*]

Cecily. Are you called Algernon?

Algernon. I cannot deny it.

Cecily. Oh!

Gwendolen. Is your name really John?

47. A deliberate echo of Jack's remark in Act 1 that "half an hour after they have met, [Cecily and Gwendolen] will be calling each other sister." The frostiness between Cecily and Gwendolen up to this point, following their discovery that they are both engaged to Ernest, similarly echoes Algernon's retort in Act 1, that women call each other sister only "when they have called each other a lot of other things first."

Jack. [*Standing rather proudly.*] I could deny it if I liked. I could deny anything if I liked. But my name certainly is John. It has been John for years.

Cecily. [*To Gwendolen.*] A gross deception has been practised on both of us.

Gwendolen. My poor wounded Cecily!

Cecily. My sweet wronged Gwendolen!

Gwendolen. [*Slowly and seriously.*] You will call me sister, will you not?[47] [*They embrace. Jack and Algernon groan and walk up and down.*]

Cecily. [*Rather brightly.*] There is just one question I would like to be allowed to ask my guardian.

Gwendolen. An admirable idea! Mr. Worthing, there is just one question I would like to be permitted to put to you. Where is your brother Ernest? We are both engaged to be married to your brother Ernest, so it is a matter of some importance to us to know where your brother Ernest is at present.

Jack. [*Slowly and hesitatingly.*] Gwendolen—Cecily—it is very painful for me to be forced to speak the truth. It is the first time in my life that I have ever been reduced to such a painful position, and I am really quite inexperienced in doing anything of the kind. However, I will tell you quite frankly that I have no brother Ernest. I have no

48. In her poem "The Happiest Girl in the World," the late-Victorian poet Augusta Webster dramatizes the thoughts of a young Victorian woman shortly after her betrothal to her future husband:

> all my life is morrow to my love.
> Oh fortunate morrow! Oh, sweet happy love!...
> ...now that I am his,
> And know if mine is love enough for him,
> And make myself believe it all is true.

> (*Portraits and Other Poems*, ed. Christine Sutphin
> [Ontario, Canada: Broadview Press, 2000], 185)

brother at all. I never had a brother in my life, and I certainly have not the smallest intention of ever having one in the future.

Cecily. [*Surprised.*] No brother at all?

Jack. [*Cheerily.*] None!

Gwendolen. [*Severely.*] Had you never a brother of any kind?

Jack. [*Pleasantly.*] Never. Not even of any kind.

Gwendolen. I am afraid it is quite clear, Cecily, that neither of us is engaged to be married to anyone.

Cecily. It is not a very pleasant position for a young girl suddenly to find herself in.[48] Is it?

Gwendolen. Let us go into the house. They will hardly venture to come after us there.

Cecily. No, men are so cowardly, aren't they? [*They retire into the house with scornful looks.*]

Jack. This ghastly state of things is what you call Bunburying, I suppose?

Algernon. Yes, and a perfectly wonderful Bunbury it is. The most wonderful Bunbury I have ever had in my life.

Jack. Well, you've no right whatsoever to Bunbury here.

49. "It is only the superficial qualities that last," Wilde observes in "Phrases and Philosophies for the Use of the Young" (*The Chameleon*, December 1894). "Man's deeper nature is soon found out."

Algernon. That is absurd. One has a right to Bunbury anywhere one chooses. Every serious Bunburyist knows that.

Jack. Serious Bunburyist! Good heavens!

Algernon. Well, one must be serious about something, if one wants to have any amusement in life. I happen to be serious about Bunburying. What on earth you are serious about I haven't got the remotest idea. About everything, I should fancy. You have such an absolutely trivial nature.[49]

Jack. Well, the only small satisfaction I have in the whole of this wretched business is that your friend Bunbury is quite exploded. You won't be able to run down to the country quite so often as you used to do, dear Algy. And a very good thing too.

Algernon. Your brother is a little off colour, isn't he, dear Jack? You won't be able to disappear to London quite so frequently as your wicked custom was. And not a bad thing either.

Jack. As for your conduct towards Miss Cardew, I must say that your taking in a sweet, simple, innocent girl like that is quite inexcusable. To say nothing of the fact that she is my ward.

Algernon. I can see no possible defence at all for your deceiving a brilliant, clever, thoroughly experienced young

lady like Miss Fairfax. To say nothing of the fact that she is my cousin.

Jack. I wanted to be engaged to Gwendolen, that is all. I love her.

Algernon. Well, I simply wanted to be engaged to Cecily. I adore her.

Jack. There is certainly no chance of your marrying Miss Cardew.

Algernon. I don't think there is much likelihood, Jack, of you and Miss Fairfax being united.

Jack. Well, that is no business of yours.

Algernon. If it was my business, I wouldn't talk about it. [*Begins to eat muffins.*] It is very vulgar to talk about one's business. Only people like stockbrokers do that, and then merely at dinner parties.

Jack. How you can sit there, calmly eating muffins when we are in this horrible trouble, I can't make out. You seem to me to be perfectly heartless.

Algernon. Well, I can't eat muffins in an agitated manner. The butter would probably get on my cuffs. One should always eat muffins quite calmly. It is the only way to eat them.

Jack. I say it's perfectly heartless your eating muffins at all, under the circumstances.

50. Algernon, who hungrily consumed all the cucumber sandwiches in Act 1, as well as a great deal of champagne before the play even started, is a compulsive eater. He implies here that his eating is a form of psychological disorder, in which oral gratifications keep at bay deeper, less easily satisfied kinds of desire. In this regard, he echoes his creator, Oscar Wilde, who was also an inveterate eater, as well as a compulsive smoker and heavy drinker, and who asks rhetorically, "who . . . in these degenerate days would hesitate between an ode and an omelette, a sonnet and a salmis?" ("Dinners and Dishes," *Pall Mall Gazette*, 7 Mar. 1885, repr. in *Journalism: Part One*, vol. 6 of *The Complete Works of Oscar Wilde*, ed. John Stokes and Mark W. Turner [Oxford: Oxford University Press, 2013], 39). For Wilde, food was intertwined with both his intellectual and his sexual life: Thomas Wright tells us that Wilde "habitually tore off the top corner of the page" of books he was reading, "then rolled the paper into a ball and put it into his mouth" (Wright, *Built of Books: How Reading Defined the Life of Oscar Wilde* [New York: Henry Holt, 2008], 154).

51. This stage direction was inserted in 1899, in place of "*They change plates.*"

Algernon. When I am in trouble, eating is the only thing that consoles me. Indeed, when I am in really great trouble, as any one who knows me intimately will tell you, I refuse everything except food and drink.[50] At the present moment I am eating muffins because I am unhappy. Besides, I am particularly fond of muffins. [*Rising.*]

Jack. [*Rising.*] Well, that is no reason why you should eat them all in that greedy way. [*Takes muffins from Algernon.*]

Algernon. [*Offering tea-cake.*] I wish you would have tea-cake instead. I don't like tea-cake.

Jack. Good heavens! I suppose a man may eat his own muffins in his own garden.

Algernon. But you have just said it was perfectly heartless to eat muffins.

Jack. I said it was perfectly heartless of you, under the circumstances. That is a very different thing.

Algernon. That may be. But the muffins are the same. [*He seizes the muffin-dish from Jack.*][51]

Jack. Algy, I wish to goodness you would go.

Algernon. You can't possibly ask me to go without having some dinner. It's absurd. I never go without my dinner. No one ever does, except vegetarians and people like that. Besides I have just made arrangements with Dr. Chasuble to be christened at a quarter to six under the name of Ernest.

Oscar Wilde, 1889. Photo by W. & D. Downey.

Mark Samuels Lasner Collection, on loan to the University of Delaware Library.

Jack. My dear fellow, the sooner you give up that nonsense the better. I made arrangements this morning with Dr. Chasuble to be christened myself at 5.30, and I naturally will take the name of Ernest. Gwendolen would wish it. We can't both be christened Ernest. It's absurd. Besides, I have a perfect right to be christened if I like. There is no evidence at all that I have ever been christened by anybody. I should think it extremely probable I never was, and so does Dr. Chasuble. It is entirely different in your case. You have been christened already.

Algernon. Yes, but I have not been christened for years.

Jack. Yes, but you have been christened. That is the important thing.

Algernon. Quite so. So I know my constitution can stand it. If you are not quite sure about your ever having been christened, I must say I think it rather dangerous your venturing on it now. It might make you very unwell. You can hardly have forgotten that some one very closely connected with you was very nearly carried off this week in Paris by a severe chill.

Jack. Yes, but you said yourself that a severe chill was not hereditary.

Algernon. It usen't to be, I know—but I daresay it is now. Science is always making wonderful improvements in things.

"Doing Bunbury in the Country," sketch, by H. P. Seppings Wright, accompanying a review of the first production, that appeared in *The Illustrated London News*, February 23, 1895. Alderman Library, University of Virginia.

Jack. [*Picking up the muffin-dish.*] Oh, that is nonsense; you are always talking nonsense.

Algernon. Jack, you are at the muffins again! I wish you wouldn't. There are only two left. [*Takes them.*] I told you I was particularly fond of muffins.

Jack. But I hate tea-cake.

Algernon. Why on earth then do you allow tea-cake to be served up for your guests? What ideas you have of hospitality!

Jack. Algernon! I have already told you to go. I don't want you here. Why don't you go!

Algernon. I haven't quite finished my tea yet! and there is still one muffin left. [*Jack groans, and sinks into a chair. Algernon still continues eating.*]

ACT-DROP

1. "I could wish that Mr. Wilde had not been quite so nice [about this morning-room]. . . . He had it painted all of a green carnation," remarked the *Sunday Times* on reviewing the first production (17 Feb. 1895), while the *Era* reported (16 Feb. 1895), "Walter Hann's morning-room for the last act was elaborately appointed and very effective" (both quoted in editorial note to *Oscar Wilde's "The Importance of Being Earnest": A Reconstructive Critical Edition*, ed. Joseph Donohue, with Ruth Berggren [Gerrards Cross, UK: Colin Smythe, 1995], 303).

2. Wilde added *"some dreadful popular air from a British Opera"* in 1899, leading many readers to understand this stage direction as a sly dig at Gilbert and Sullivan. Joseph Donohue states that "in modern productions . . . the whistled tune is often 'I am the Captain of the Pinafore' or 'When I was a Lad' [from Gilbert's and Sullivan's *H.M.S. Pinafore*]" (Donohue, editorial note to *Oscar Wilde's "The Importance of Being Earnest,"* 304). However, in the first production, according to Donohue, the actors whistled "Home, Sweet Home," from Henry Bishop's 1823 opera *Clari, or the Maid of Milan* (ibid.).

ACT THREE

SCENE: Morning-room at the Manor House. Gwendolen and Cecily are at the window, looking out into the garden.[1]

Gwendolen. The fact that they did not follow us at once into the house, as any one else would have done, seems to me to show that they have some sense of shame left.

Cecily. They have been eating muffins. That looks like repentance.

Gwendolen. [*After a pause.*] They don't seem to notice us at all. Couldn't you cough?

Cecily. But I haven't got a cough.

Gwendolen. They're looking at us. What effrontery!

Cecily. They're approaching. That's very forward of them.

Gwendolen. Let us preserve a dignified silence.

Cecily. Certainly. It's the only thing to do now.

[*Enter Jack followed by Algernon. They whistle some dreadful popular air from a British Opera.*][2]

3. Wilde had used an earlier version of this famous epigram in "Phrases and Philosophies for the Use of the Young" (*Chameleon*, December 1894).

Gwendolen. This dignified silence seems to produce an unpleasant effect.

Cecily. A most distasteful one.

Gwendolen. But we will not be the first to speak.

Cecily. Certainly not.

Gwendolen. Mr. Worthing, I have something very particular to ask you. Much depends on your reply.

Cecily. Gwendolen, your common sense is invaluable. Mr. Moncrieff, kindly answer me the following question. Why did you pretend to be my guardian's brother?

Algernon. In order that I might have an opportunity of meeting you.

Cecily. [*To Gwendolen.*] That certainly seems a satisfactory explanation, does it not?

Gwendolen. Yes, dear, if you can believe him.

Cecily. I don't. But that does not affect the wonderful beauty of his answer.

Gwendolen. True. In matters of grave importance, style, not sincerity is the vital thing.[3] Mr. Worthing, what explanation can you offer to me for pretending to have a brother? Was it in order that you might have an opportunity of coming up to town to see me as often as possible?

4. Wilde added "This is not the moment for scepticism" when preparing copy for the 1899 edition, later changing this to "German scepticism." He may have been thinking of his comment, in "The Critic as Artist," "Like Goethe after he had read Kant . . . we desire the concrete, and nothing but the concrete can satisfy us" (*Criticism*, ed. Josephine M. Guy, vol. 4 of *The Complete Works of Oscar Wilde* [Oxford: Oxford University Press, 2007], 176), or perhaps of his comment, "Kant annihilated metaphysics" and "brought speculation back to man" (Wilde, *Oscar Wilde's Oxford Notebooks*, ed. Philip E. Smith and Michael S. Helfand [Oxford: Oxford University Press, 1989], 148, 150). But Wilde may have been thinking too of how thoroughly German academic philology had demolished literal belief in the gospels, in favor of more relativistic and historical modes of understanding.

Jack. Can you doubt it, Miss Fairfax?

Gwendolen. I have the gravest doubts upon the subject. But I intend to crush them. This is not the moment for German scepticism.[4] [*Moving to Cecily.*] Their explanations appear to be quite satisfactory, especially Mr. Worthing's. That seems to me to have the stamp of truth upon it.

Cecily. I am more than content with what Mr. Moncrieff said. His voice alone inspires one with absolute credulity.

Gwendolen. Then you think we should forgive them?

Cecily. Yes. I mean no.

Gwendolen. True! I had forgotten. There are principles at stake that one cannot surrender. Which of us should tell them? The task is not a pleasant one.

Cecily. Could we not both speak at the same time?

Gwendolen. An excellent idea! I nearly always speak at the same time as other people. Will you take the time from me?

Cecily. Certainly. [*Gwendolen beats time with uplifted finger.*]

Gwendolen and **Cecily** [*Speaking together.*] Your Christian names are still an insuperable barrier. That is all!

Jack and **Algernon** [*Speaking together.*] Our Christian names! Is that all? But we are going to be christened this afternoon.

5. Although women did not receive the right to vote in Britain until 1918, the movement for sexual equality was extremely active in late-Victorian Britain, especially after the publication of John Stuart Mill's *The Subjection of Women* in 1869. Wilde had himself commissioned and edited articles titled "The Position of Woman" and "The Fallacy of the Superiority of Man" while editor of *Woman's World*. And in *A Woman of No Importance* (1893), he writes that "the growing influence of women is the one reassuring thing in our political life" (Act 1, *A Woman of No Importance*, in *Complete Works of Oscar Wilde*, ed. Merlin Holland, rev. ed. [London: Harper Collins, 1994], 469).

Gwendolen. [*To Jack.*] For my sake you are prepared to do this terrible thing?

Jack. I am.

Cecily. [*To Algernon.*] To please me you are ready to face this fearful ordeal?

Algernon. I am!

Gwendolen. How absurd to talk of the equality of the sexes![5] Where questions of self-sacrifice are concerned, men are infinitely beyond us.

Jack. We are. [*Clasps hands with Algernon.*]

Cecily. They have moments of physical courage of which we women know absolutely nothing.

Gwendolen. [*To Jack.*] Darling!

Algernon. [*To Cecily.*] Darling! [*They fall into each other's arms.*]

[*Enter Merriman. When he enters he coughs loudly, seeing the situation.*]

Merriman. Ahem! Ahem! Lady Bracknell!

Jack. Good heavens!

[*Enter Lady Bracknell. The couples separate in alarm. Exit Merriman.*]

6. A slow, heavy train, dedicated principally to the transport of personal and commercial goods, with sparse accommodations for paying passengers. Lady Bracknell would normally travel first-class in a passenger or express train.

7. The object of Wilde's satire here is complex. The University Extension Scheme, whereby English universities offered free lectures to unenrolled students in the principal cities, was of particular importance to women, who, with few exceptions, had no access to formal higher education. Wilde's title for the "unusually lengthy lecture"—added only just before publication in 1899—satirizes the stultifying and conservative effects of wealth, though it might also allude, albeit unconsciously, to the crushing poverty that played a part in diminishing Wilde's own creative powers after his release from jail in 1897.

8. "Indeed I have never undeceived him on any question. I would consider it wrong" was added in 1899.

Lady Bracknell. Gwendolen! What does this mean?

Gwendolen. Merely that I am engaged to be married to Mr. Worthing, mamma.

Lady Bracknell. Come here. Sit down. Sit down immediately. Hesitation of any kind is a sign of mental decay in the young, of physical weakness in the old. [*Turns to Jack.*] Apprised, sir, of my daughter's sudden flight by her trusty maid, whose confidence I purchased by means of a small coin, I followed her at once by a luggage train.[6] Her unhappy father is, I am glad to say, under the impression that she is attending a more than usually lengthy lecture by the University Extension Scheme on the Influence of a permanent income on Thought.[7] I do not propose to undeceive him. Indeed I have never undeceived him on any question. I would consider it wrong.[8] But of course, you will clearly understand that all communication between yourself and my daughter must cease immediately from this moment. On this point, as indeed on all points, I am firm.

Jack. I am engaged to be married to Gwendolen, Lady Bracknell!

Lady Bracknell. You are nothing of the kind, sir. And now, as regards Algernon! . . . Algernon!

Algernon. Yes, Aunt Augusta.

Lady Bracknell. May I ask if it is in this house that your invalid friend Mr. Bunbury resides?

9. This witty line of dialogue, containing Lady Bracknell's response to the idea that Bunbury had been "exploded," was inserted only in 1899, together with the beginning of Algernon's next speech ("My dear Aunt Augusta"). Fears of revolutionary violence were acute in Wilde's day, when many revolutionaries exploited Alfred Nobel's invention of dynamite (1863) to promote violence against political or symbolic enemies. Such violence, and the fear it aroused in England, provided the basis for Wilde's first play, *Vera, or The Nihilists* (1880) and was later satirized by Wilde in "Lord Arthur Savile's Crime" (1887).

Algernon. [*Stammering.*] Oh! No! Bunbury doesn't live here. Bunbury is somewhere else at present. In fact, Bunbury is dead.

Lady Bracknell. Dead! When did Mr. Bunbury die? His death must have been extremely sudden.

Algernon. [*Airily.*] Oh! I killed Bunbury this afternoon. I mean poor Bunbury died this afternoon.

Lady Bracknell. What did he die of?

Algernon. Bunbury? Oh, he was quite exploded.

Lady Bracknell. Exploded! Was he the victim of a revolutionary outrage? I was not aware that Mr. Bunbury was interested in social legislation. If so, he is well punished for his morbidity.[9]

Algernon. My dear Aunt Augusta, I mean he was found out! The doctors found out that Bunbury could not live, that is what I mean—so Bunbury died.

Lady Bracknell. He seems to have had great confidence in the opinion of his physicians. I am glad, however, that he made up his mind at the last to some definite course of action, and acted under proper medical advice. And now that we have finally got rid of this Mr. Bunbury, may I ask, Mr. Worthing, who is that young person whose hand my nephew Algernon is now holding in what seems to me a peculiarly unnecessary manner?

10. See *Oxford English Dictionary,* s.v. "sporran": "A pouch or large purse made of skin, usually with the hair left on and with ornamental tassels, etc., worn in front of the kilt by Scottish Highlanders." Wilde originally wrote "the Glen" but changed this to "the Sporran" in preparing the 1899 edition.

11. "S.W." is still the postal code for districts southwest of the center of London; "N.B.," meaning North Britain, was the Victorian postal code for Scotland.

Jack. That lady is Miss Cecily Cardew, my ward.

[*Lady Bracknell bows coldly to Cecily.*]

Algernon. I am engaged to be married to Cecily, Aunt Augusta.

Lady Bracknell. I beg your pardon?

Cecily. Mr. Moncrieff and I are engaged to be married, Lady Bracknell.

Lady Bracknell. [*With a shiver, crossing to the sofa and sitting down.*] I do not know whether there is anything peculiarly exciting in the air of this particular part of Hertfordshire, but the number of engagements that go on seems to me considerably above the proper average that statistics have laid down for our guidance. I think some preliminary inquiry on my part would not be out of place. Mr. Worthing, is Miss Cardew at all connected with any of the larger railway stations in London? I merely desire information. Until yesterday I had no idea that there were any families or persons whose origin was a Terminus. [*Jack looks perfectly furious, but restrains himself.*]

Jack. [*In a clear, cold voice.*] Miss Cardew is the granddaughter of the late Mr. Thomas Cardew of 149 Belgrave Square, S.W.; Gervase Park, Dorking, Surrey; and the Sporran,[10] Fifeshire, N.B.[11]

12. "even in tradesmen" was added in 1899.

13. Either *The Royal Blue Book, The Royal Court Guide and Fashion-able Directory*, or *Boyle's Fashionable Court & Country Guide, and Town Visiting Directory.* These were "Society" directories—directories of the fashionable, wealthy, and well-connected—published and updated on a regular basis.

14. lawyers

Lady Bracknell. That sounds not unsatisfactory. Three addresses always inspire confidence, even in tradesmen.[12] But what proof have I of their authenticity?

Jack. I have carefully preserved the Court Guides of the period.[13] They are open to your inspection, Lady Bracknell.

Lady Bracknell. [*Grimly.*] I have known strange errors in that publication.

Jack. Miss Cardew's family solicitors[14] are Messrs. Markby, Markby, and Markby.

Lady Bracknell. Markby, Markby, and Markby? A firm of the very highest position in their profession. Indeed I am told that one of the Mr. Markbys is occasionally to be seen at dinner parties. So far I am satisfied.

Jack. [*Very irritably.*] How extremely kind of you, Lady Bracknell! I have also in my possession, you will be pleased to hear, certificates of Miss Cardew's birth, baptism, whooping cough, registration, vaccination, confirmation, and the measles; both the German and the English variety.

Lady Bracknell. Ah! A life crowded with incident, I see; though perhaps somewhat too exciting for a young girl. I am not myself in favour of premature experiences. [*Rises, looks at her watch.*] Gwendolen! the time approaches for our departure. We have not a moment to lose. As a matter of

15. Government bonds, producing a steady stream of income. Cecily's fortune is at once immense, safe, and remunerative.

16. "So pleased to have seen you" was added in 1899.

17. "If the poor only had profiles," Wilde writes in "Phrases and Philosophies for the Use of the Young" (*The Chameleon*, December 1894), "there would be no difficulty in solving the problem of poverty."

form, Mr. Worthing, I had better ask you if Miss Cardew has any little fortune?

Jack. Oh! about a hundred and thirty thousand pounds in the Funds.[15] That is all. Goodbye, Lady Bracknell. So pleased to have seen you.[16]

Lady Bracknell. [*Sitting down again.*] A moment, Mr. Worthing. A hundred and thirty thousand pounds! And in the Funds! Miss Cardew seems to me a most attractive young lady, now that I look at her. Few girls of the present day have any really solid qualities, any of the qualities that last, and improve with time. We live, I regret to say, in an age of surfaces. [*To Cecily.*] Come over here, dear. [*Cecily goes across.*] Pretty child! your dress is sadly simple, and your hair seems almost as Nature might have left it. But we can soon alter all that. A thoroughly experienced French maid produces a really marvellous result in a very brief space of time. I remember recommending one to young Lady Lancing, and after three months her own husband did not know her.

Jack. [*Aside.*] And after six months nobody knew her.

Lady Bracknell. [*Glares at Jack for a few moments. Then bends, with a practised smile, to Cecily.*] Kindly turn round, sweet child. [*Cecily turns completely round.*] No, the side view is what I want. [*Cecily presents her profile.*] Yes, quite as I expected. There are distinct social possibilities in your profile. The two weak points in our age are its want of principle and its want of profile.[17] The chin a little higher,

Wilde and Douglas in Naples, following Wilde's release from prison, late 1897. The William Andrews Clark Memorial Library, University of California, Los Angeles.

dear. Style largely depends on the way the chin is worn. They are worn very high, just at present. Algernon!

Algernon. Yes, Aunt Augusta!

Lady Bracknell. There are distinct social possibilities in Miss Cardew's profile.

Algernon. Cecily is the sweetest, dearest, prettiest girl in the whole world. And I don't care twopence about social possibilities.

Lady Bracknell. Never speak disrespectfully of Society, Algernon. Only people who can't get into it do that. [*To Cecily.*] Dear child, of course you know that Algernon has nothing but his debts to depend upon. But I do not approve of mercenary marriages. When I married Lord Bracknell I had no fortune of any kind. But I never dreamed for a moment of allowing that to stand in my way. Well, I suppose I must give my consent.

Algernon. Thank you, Aunt Augusta.

Lady Bracknell. Cecily, you may kiss me!

Cecily. [*Kisses her.*] Thank you, Lady Bracknell.

Lady Bracknell. You may also address me as Aunt Augusta for the future.

Cecily. Thank you, Aunt Augusta.

Lady Bracknell. The marriage, I think, had better take place quite soon.

18. "He is an Oxonian" was added in 1899. An Oxonian is a graduate of Oxford University—and thus, for Victorians, an impeccable gentleman.

Algernon. Thank you, Aunt Augusta.

Cecily. Thank you, Aunt Augusta.

Lady Bracknell. To speak frankly, I am not in favour of long engagements. They give people the opportunity of finding out each other's character before marriage, which I think is never advisable.

Jack. I beg your pardon for interrupting you, Lady Bracknell, but this engagement is quite out of the question. I am Miss Cardew's guardian, and she cannot marry without my consent until she comes of age. That consent I absolutely decline to give.

Lady Bracknell. Upon what grounds may I ask? Algernon is an extremely, I may almost say an ostentatiously, eligible young man. He has nothing, but he looks everything. What more can one desire?

Jack. It pains me very much to have to speak frankly to you, Lady Bracknell, about your nephew, but the fact is that I do not approve at all of his moral character. I suspect him of being untruthful. [*Algernon and Cecily look at him in indignant amazement.*]

Lady Bracknell. Untruthful! My nephew Algernon? Impossible! He is an Oxonian.[18]

Jack. I fear there can be no possible doubt about the matter. This afternoon during my temporary absence in London on an important question of romance, he obtained admission

19. A fine vintage champagne, inserted in 1899 in place of " '74 champagne."

to my house by means of the false pretence of being my brother. Under an assumed name he drank, I've just been informed by my butler, an entire pint bottle of my Perrier-Jouet, Brut, '89;[19] a wine I was specially reserving for myself. Continuing his disgraceful deception, he succeeded in the course of the afternoon in alienating the affections of my only ward. He subsequently stayed to tea, and devoured every single muffin. And what makes his conduct all the more heartless is, that he was perfectly well aware from the first that I have no brother, that I never had a brother, and that I don't intend to have a brother, not even of any kind. I distinctly told him so myself yesterday afternoon.

Lady Bracknell. Ahem! Mr. Worthing, after careful consideration I have decided entirely to overlook my nephew's conduct to you.

Jack. That is very generous of you, Lady Bracknell. My own decision, however, is unalterable. I decline to give my consent.

Lady Bracknell. [*To Cecily.*] Come here, sweet child. [*Cecily goes over.*] How old are you, dear?

Cecily. Well, I am really only eighteen, but I always admit to twenty when I go to evening parties.

Lady Bracknell. You are perfectly right in making some slight alteration. Indeed, no woman should ever be quite accurate about her age. It looks so calculating . . . [*In a meditative manner.*] Eighteen, but admitting to twenty at evening parties.

20. "Punctuality is the thief of time," Wilde observes in *The Picture of Dorian Gray*, in an adaptation of Edward Young's aphorism "Procrastination is the Thief of Time" (*The Picture of Dorian Gray: An Annotated, Uncensored Edition*, 109).

Well, it will not be very long before you are of age and free from the restraints of tutelage. So I don't think your guardian's consent is, after all, a matter of any importance.

Jack. Pray excuse me, Lady Bracknell, for interrupting you again, but it is only fair to tell you that according to the terms of her grandfather's will Miss Cardew does not come legally of age till she is thirty-five.

Lady Bracknell. That does not seem to me to be a grave objection. Thirty-five is a very attractive age. London society is full of women of the very highest birth who have, of their own free choice, remained thirty-five for years. Lady Dumbleton is an instance in point. To my own knowledge she has been thirty-five ever since she arrived at the age of forty, which was many years ago now. I see no reason why our dear Cecily should not be even still more attractive at the age you mention than she is at present. There will be a large accumulation of property.

Cecily. Algy, could you wait for me till I was thirty-five?

Algernon. Of course I could, Cecily. You know I could.

Cecily. Yes, I felt it instinctively, but I couldn't wait all that time. I hate waiting even five minutes for anybody. It always makes me rather cross. I am not punctual myself, I know, but I do like punctuality in others,[20] and waiting, even to be married, is quite out of the question.

Algernon. Then what is to be done, Cecily?

Cecily. I don't know, Mr. Moncrieff.

Lady Bracknell. My dear Mr. Worthing, as Miss Cardew states positively that she cannot wait till she is thirty-five—a remark which I am bound to say seems to me to show a somewhat impatient nature—I would beg of you to reconsider your decision.

Jack. But my dear Lady Bracknell, the matter is entirely in your own hands. The moment you consent to my marriage with Gwendolen, I will most gladly allow your nephew to form an alliance with my ward.

Lady Bracknell. [*Rising and drawing herself up.*] You must be quite aware that what you propose is out of the question.

Jack. Then a passionate celibacy is all that any of us can look forward to.

Lady Bracknell. That is not the destiny I propose for Gwendolen. Algernon, of course, can choose for himself. [*Pulls out her watch.*] Come, dear; [*Gwendolen rises*] we have already missed five, if not six, trains. To miss any more might expose us to comment on the platform.

[*Enter Dr. Chasuble.*]

Chasuble. Everything is quite ready for the christenings.

Lady Bracknell. The christenings, sir! Is not that somewhat premature?

21. Anabaptists, a sect of dissenting Protestants active in Germany in the sixteenth century, rejected infant baptism and required believers to be "re-baptized" as adults while making an active confession of faith. In Wilde's day, the term *anabaptist* was "applied (more or less opprobriously) to the Protestant religious body called Baptists [and] also, somewhat loosely, to other rejecters of Anglican doctrine as to the sacraments and 'holy orders'" (*Oxford English Dictionary*, s.v. "anabaptist"). As an adherent to Anglican doctrine, Chasuble means *anabaptist* in this second, looser sense. Wilde added this witty sentence only in 1899, along with the beginning of the next ("However, as your present mood seems to be one peculiarly secular").

Chasuble. [*Looking rather puzzled, and pointing to Jack and Algernon.*] Both these gentlemen have expressed a desire for immediate baptism.

Lady Bracknell. At their age? The idea is grotesque and irreligious! Algernon, I forbid you to be baptised. I will not hear of such excesses. Lord Bracknell would be highly displeased if he learned that that was the way in which you wasted your time and money.

Chasuble. Am I to understand then that there are to be no christenings at all this afternoon?

Jack. I don't think that, as things are now, it would be of much practical value to either of us, Dr. Chasuble.

Chasuble. I am grieved to hear such sentiments from you, Mr. Worthing. They savour of the heretical views of the Anabaptists,[21] views that I have completely refuted in four of my unpublished sermons. However, as your present mood seems to be one peculiarly secular, I will return to the church at once. Indeed, I have just been informed by the pew-opener that for the last hour and a half Miss Prism has been waiting for me in the vestry.

Lady Bracknell. [*Starting.*] Miss Prism! Did I hear you mention a Miss Prism?

Chasuble. Yes, Lady Bracknell. I am on my way to join her.

Lady Bracknell. Pray allow me to detain you for a moment. This matter may prove to be one of vital importance to Lord

22. A confirmed bachelor. Chasuble misconstrues Lady Bracknell as asking whether Miss Prism is his mistress or "kept woman." But this misconstrual, as well as the severity of Chasuble's reply, is a clue to his subconscious desire for Prism.

23. "In spite of what I hear of her" was added in 1899.

Bracknell and myself. Is this Miss Prism a female of repellent aspect, remotely connected with education?

Chasuble. [*Somewhat indignantly.*] She is the most cultivated of ladies, and the very picture of respectability.

Lady Bracknell. It is obviously the same person. May I ask what position she holds in your household?

Chasuble. [*Severely.*] I am a celibate,[22] madam.

Jack. [*Interposing.*] Miss Prism, Lady Bracknell, has been for the last three years Miss Cardew's esteemed governess and valued companion.

Lady Bracknell. In spite of what I hear of her,[23] I must see her at once. Let her be sent for.

Chasuble. [*Looking off.*] She approaches; she is nigh.

[*Enter Miss Prism hurriedly.*]

Miss Prism. I was told you expected me in the vestry, dear Canon. I have been waiting for you there for an hour and three-quarters. [*Catches sight of Lady Bracknell, who has fixed her with a stony glare. Miss Prism grows pale and quails. She looks anxiously round as if desirous to escape.*]

Lady Bracknell. [*In a severe, judicial voice.*] Prism! [*Miss Prism bows her head in shame.*] Come here, Prism! [*Miss Prism approaches in a humble manner.*] Prism! Where is that baby?

24. A baby carriage or "pram," from which the modern baby buggy, pushchair, or stroller descends.

25. An area to the west of Central London, substituted in 1899 for the distinctly more fashionable "Hyde Park." According to H. G. Wells, who reviewed the first performance, the location of the abandoned perambulator was rendered as "the summit of Primrose Hill" on the opening night (unsigned review, *Pall Mall Gazette*, 15 Feb. 1895, repr. in *Oscar Wilde: The Critical Heritage*, ed. Karl Beckson (London: Routledge and Kegan Paul, 1970), 188.

26. The part of the perambulator accommodating the baby.

[*General consternation. The Canon starts back in horror. Algernon and Jack pretend to be anxious to shield Cecily and Gwendolen from hearing the details of a terrible public scandal.*] Twenty-eight years ago, Prism, you left Lord Bracknell's house, Number 104, Upper Grosvenor Street, in charge of a perambulator[24] that contained a baby of the male sex. You never returned. A few weeks later, through the elaborate investigations of the Metropolitan police, the perambulator was discovered at midnight, standing by itself in a remote corner of Bayswater.[25] It contained the manuscript of a three-volume novel of more than usually revolting sentimentality. [*Miss Prism starts in involuntary indignation.*] But the baby was not there! [*Every one looks at Miss Prism.*] Prism! Where is that baby? [*A pause.*]

Miss Prism. Lady Bracknell, I admit with shame that I do not know. I only wish I did. The plain facts of the case are these. On the morning of the day you mention, a day that is for ever branded on my memory, I prepared as usual to take the baby out in its perambulator. I had also with me a somewhat old, but capacious hand-bag in which I had intended to place the manuscript of a work of fiction that I had written during my few unoccupied hours. In a moment of mental abstraction, for which I never can forgive myself, I deposited the manuscript in the bassinette,[26] and placed the baby in the hand-bag.

Jack. [*Who has been listening attentively.*] But where did you deposit the hand-bag?

Miss Prism. Do not ask me, Mr. Worthing.

Jack. Miss Prism, this is a matter of no small importance to me. I insist on knowing where you deposited the hand-bag that contained that infant.

Miss Prism. I left it in the cloak-room of one of the larger railway stations in London.

Jack. What railway station?

Miss Prism. [*Quite crushed.*] Victoria. The Brighton line. [*Sinks into a chair.*]

Jack. I must retire to my room for a moment. Gwendolen, wait here for me.

Gwendolen. If you are not too long, I will wait here for you all my life.

[*Exit Jack in great excitement.*]

Chasuble. What do you think this means, Lady Bracknell?

Lady Bracknell. I dare not even suspect, Dr. Chasuble. I need hardly tell you that in families of high position strange coincidences are not supposed to occur. They are hardly considered the thing.

[*Noises heard overhead as if some one was throwing trunks about. Every one looks up.*]

Cecily. Uncle Jack seems strangely agitated.

27. Horse-drawn omnibus—ancestor of the modern metropolitan bus—terminating at Gower Street in Central London. That Miss Prism travels by omnibus, whereas the other characters of the play travel by train, is a mark of her lower social and economic standing.

28. A temperance beverage is a nonalcoholic beverage. Although once fashionable, Leamington (short for Leamington Spa, in Warwickshire) had by Wilde's day declined in popularity and had become—like Tunbridge Wells, mentioned in Act 1—a place of retirement for the elderly and the infirm.

Chasuble. Your guardian has a very emotional nature.

Lady Bracknell. This noise is extremely unpleasant. It sounds as if he was having an argument. I dislike arguments of any kind. They are always vulgar, and often convincing.

Chasuble. [*Looking up.*] It has stopped now. [*The noise is redoubled.*]

Lady Bracknell. I wish he would arrive at some conclusion.

Gwendolen. This suspense is terrible. I hope it will last. [*Enter Jack with a hand-bag of black leather in his hand.*]

Jack. [*Rushing over to Miss Prism.*] Is this the hand-bag, Miss Prism? Examine it carefully before you speak. The happiness of more than one life depends on your answer.

Miss Prism. [*Calmly.*] It seems to be mine. Yes, here is the injury it received through the upsetting of a Gower Street omnibus[27] in younger and happier days. Here is the stain on the lining caused by the explosion of a temperance beverage, an incident that occurred at Leamington.[28] And here, on the lock, are my initials. I had forgotten that in an extravagant mood I had had them placed there. The bag is undoubtedly mine. I am delighted to have it so unexpectedly restored to me. It has been a great inconvenience being without it all these years.

Jack. [*In a pathetic voice.*] Miss Prism, more is restored to you than this hand-bag. I was the baby you placed in it.

29. Jack's phrase echoes Christ's injunction, on being asked to judge the woman taken in adultery, "He that is without sin among you, let him first cast a stone at her" (John 8:7). Wilde changed "throw" to "cast," thus giving the line its present form, in 1899.

Miss Prism. [*Amazed.*] You?

Jack. [*Embracing her.*] Yes . . . mother!

Miss Prism. [*Recoiling in indignant astonishment.*] Mr. Worthing! I am unmarried!

Jack. Unmarried! I do not deny that is a serious blow. But after all, who has the right to cast a stone against one who has suffered?[29] Cannot repentance wipe out an act of folly? Why should there be one law for men, and another for women? Mother, I forgive you. [*Tries to embrace her again.*]

Miss Prism. [*Still more indignant.*] Mr. Worthing, there is some error. [*Pointing to Lady Bracknell.*] There is the lady who can tell you who you really are.

Jack. [*After a pause.*] Lady Bracknell, I hate to seem inquisitive, but would you kindly inform me who I am?

Lady Bracknell. I am afraid that the news I have to give you will not altogether please you. You are the son of my poor sister, Mrs. Moncrieff, and consequently Algernon's elder brother.

Jack. Algy's elder brother! Then I have a brother after all. I knew I had a brother! I always said I had a brother! Cecily,—how could you have ever doubted that I had a brother? [*Seizes hold of Algernon.*] Dr. Chasuble, my unfortunate brother. Miss Prism, my unfortunate brother.

30. "I did my best, however, though I was out of practice" was added
in 1899.

Gwendolen, my unfortunate brother. Algy, you young scoundrel, you will have to treat me with more respect in the future. You have never behaved to me like a brother in all your life.

Algernon. Well, not till to-day, old boy, I admit. I did my best, however, though I was out of practice.[30] [*Shakes hands.*]

Gwendolen. [*To Jack.*] My own! But what own are you? What is your Christian name, now that you have become some one else?

Jack. Good heavens! . . . I had quite forgotten that point. Your decision on the subject of my name is irrevocable, I suppose?

Gwendolen. I never change, except in my affections.

Cecily. What a noble nature you have, Gwendolen!

Jack. Then the question had better be cleared up at once. Aunt Augusta, a moment. At the time when Miss Prism left me in the hand-bag, had I been christened already?

Lady Bracknell. Every luxury that money could buy, including christening, had been lavished on you by your fond and doting parents.

Jack. Then I was christened! That is settled. Now, what name was I given? Let me know the worst.

31. The last three sentences of this speech, from "He was eccentric" to "things of that kind," were added in 1899. Earlier texts have, "Your poor dear mother always addressed him as 'General.' That I remember perfectly. Indeed, I don't think she would have dared to call him by his Christian name. But I have no doubt he *had* one. He was violent in his manner, but there was nothing eccentric about him."

32. *The Official Army List*, a quarterly publication listing all the members of the British army.

33. An in-joke, added to the text, out of alphabetical order along with "Magley," in 1899; "Maxbohm" is a condensation of the name of Max Beerbohm, Wilde's fellow dandy and wit, who was present at the first performance and pronounced this scene "one of the funniest... ever written" (Richard Ellmann, *Oscar Wilde* [New York: Knopf, 1988], 430).

Lady Bracknell. Being the eldest son you were naturally christened after your father.

Jack. [*Irritably.*] Yes, but what was my father's Christian name?

Lady Bracknell. [*Meditatively.*] I cannot at the present moment recall what the General's Christian name was. But I have no doubt he had one. He was eccentric, I admit. But only in later years. And that was the result of the Indian climate, and marriage, and indigestion, and other things of that kind.[31]

Jack. Algy! Can't you recollect what our father's Christian name was?

Algernon. My dear boy, we were never even on speaking terms. He died before I was a year old.

Jack. His name would appear in the Army Lists[32] of the period, I suppose, Aunt Augusta?

Lady Bracknell. The General was essentially a man of peace, except in his domestic life. But I have no doubt his name would appear in any military directory.

Jack. The Army Lists of the last forty years are here. These delightful records should have been my constant study. [*Rushes to bookcase and tears the books out.*] M. Generals . . . Mallam, Maxbohm,[33] Magley, what ghastly names

they have—Markby, Migsby, Mobbs, Moncrieff! Lieutenant 1840, Captain, Lieutenant-Colonel, Colonel, General 1869, Christian names, Ernest John. [*Puts book very quietly down and speaks quite calmly.*] I always told you, Gwendolen, my name was Ernest, didn't I? Well, it is Ernest after all. I mean it naturally is Ernest.

Lady Bracknell. Yes, I remember now that the General was called Ernest. I knew I had some particular reason for disliking the name.

Gwendolen. Ernest! My own Ernest! I felt from the first that you could have no other name!

Jack. Gwendolen, it is a terrible thing for a man to find out suddenly that all his life he has been speaking nothing but the truth. Can you forgive me?

Gwendolen. I can. For I feel that you are sure to change.

Jack. My own one!

Chasuble. [*To Miss Prism.*] Lætitia! [*Embraces her.*]

Miss Prism. [*Enthusiastically.*] Frederick! At last!

Algernon. Cecily! [*Embraces her.*] At last!

Jack. Gwendolen! [*Embraces her.*] At last!

Lady Bracknell. My nephew, you seem to be displaying signs of triviality.

34. This famous concluding line only attained its present form at the proof stages in 1899, when Wilde added "vital" before "Importance of Being Earnest" and also inserted "signs of" before "triviality," in Lady Bracknell's preceding speech.

35. The tableau was a convention of the Victorian theater, whereby the actors momentarily "froze," holding their positions at the play's end, thereby pointing up the significance, as well as the artifice, of the conclusion.

Jack. On the contrary, Aunt Augusta, I've now realised for the first time in my life the vital Importance of Being Earnest.[34]

TABLEAU[35]

CURTAIN

Further Reading

Aquien, Pascal, and Xavier Giudicelli, eds. *The Importance of Being Earnest D'Oscar Wilde*. Paris: Presses de l'université Paris-Sorbonne, 2014.

Beckson, Karl, ed. *Oscar Wilde: The Critical Heritage*. London: Routledge and Kegan Paul, 1970.

Booth, Michael R. *Prefaces to English Nineteenth-Century Theatre*. Manchester: Manchester University Press, 1980.

Degroisse, Élodie. *The Paradox of Identity: Oscar Wilde's The Importance of Being Earnest*. Paris: Presses universitaires de France, 2014.

Eells, Emily, ed. *Wilde in Earnest*. Nanterre: Presses universitaires de Paris Ouest, 2015.

Ellmann, Richard. *Oscar Wilde*. New York: Knopf, 1988.

———, ed. *Oscar Wilde: A Collection of Critical Essays*. 1969. Reprint, Englewood Cliffs, NJ: Prentice Hall, 1986.

Eltis, Sos. *Revising Wilde: Society and Subversion in the Plays of Oscar Wilde*. Oxford, UK: Clarendon, 1996.

Gagnier, Regenia, ed. *Critical Essays on Oscar Wilde*. New York: G. K. Hall, 1991. Esp. part 2 ("Wildean Wit: *The Importance of Being Earnest*"), 93–157.

———. *Idylls of the Marketplace: Oscar Wilde and the Victorian Public*. Stanford, CA: Stanford University Press, 1986.

Kaplan, Joel, and Sheila Stowell, *Theatre and Fashion: Oscar Wilde to the Suffragettes*. Cambridge: Cambridge University Press, 1994.

McCormack, Jerusha, ed. *Wilde the Irishman.* New Haven, CT: Yale University Press, 1998.

McKenna, Neil. *The Secret Life of Oscar Wilde.* New York: Basic Books, 2005.

Modern Drama 37, no. 1 (Spring 1994, special issue).

Powell, Kerry. *Acting Wilde.* Cambridge: Cambridge University Press, 2000.

———. *Oscar Wilde and the Theatre of the 1890s.* Cambridge: Cambridge University Press, 1990.

Raby, Peter, ed. *The Cambridge Companion to Oscar Wilde.* Cambridge: Cambridge University Press, 1997.

———. *The Importance of Being Earnest: A Reader's Companion.* New York: Twayne, 1995.

Raby, Peter, and Kerry Powell, eds. *Oscar Wilde in Context.* Cambridge: Cambridge University Press, 2013.

Sandulescu, C. George, ed. *Rediscovering Oscar Wilde.* Gerrards Cross, UK: Colin Smythe, 1994.

Stephens, John Russell. *The Profession of the Playwright: British Theatre, 1800–1900.* Cambridge: Cambridge University Press, 1992.

Tydeman, William, ed. *Wilde Comedies: A Casebook.* London: Macmillan, 1982.

Wilde, Oscar. *The Complete Letters of Oscar Wilde.* Edited by Merlin Holland and Rupert Hart-Davis. New York: Henry Holt, 2000.

———. *The Definitive Four-Act Version of The Importance of Being Earnest.* Edited by Ruth Berggren. New York: Vanguard, 1987.

———. *The Importance of Being Earnest.* Edited by Russell Jackson. 1980. Reprint, London and New York: A. C. Black / Norton, 1988.

———. *The Importance of Being Earnest.* Edited by Samuel Lyndon Gladden. Peterborough, ON: Broadview, 2010.

———. *The Importance of Being Earnest and Related Writings.* Edited by Joseph Bristow. London and New York: Routledge, 1992.

———. *Oscar Wilde's "The Importance of Being Earnest": A Reconstructive Critical Edition of the First Production.* Edited by Joseph Donohue, with Ruth Berggren. Gerrards Cross, UK: Colin Smythe, 1995.

———. *The Importance of Being Earnest: A Trivial Comedy for Serious People in Four Acts as Originally Written by Oscar Wilde.* Edited by Sarah Augusta Dickson. 2 vols. New York: New York Public Library, 1956.

Worth, Katherine. *Oscar Wilde.* London: Macmillan, 1983.

Acknowledgments

It is a pleasure to acknowledge the generosity with which friends, colleagues, the publisher's readers, and above all my astute and discerning editor, John Kulka, helped refine this book during its genesis, prompting me to polish—and in some cases completely rethink—my earliest ideas. Susan Barstow, Chip Tucker, Betsy Tucker, David Latané, and Kate Nash also commented incisively on early drafts. I owe a great deal as well to three anonymous publisher's readers, and to the lively students in my Oscar Wilde seminars, especially Alex Jones. No scholar of *The Importance of Being Earnest* can afford to ignore the fine work of Joseph Donohue, now entering its fifth productive decade: my annotations and notes give a sense of my intellectual debts to him; but Joe is a picture of generosity when it comes to matters of practical help too, and I want gratefully to acknowledge his assistance, as well as that of Mark Samuels Lasner.

I would also like to acknowledge, with profound gratitude, the support my work consistently receives at Virginia Commonwealth University, particularly from James Coleman, dean of humanities and sciences, and Katherine Bassard, chair of English. They and their staff fight valiantly to support literary research, notwithstanding the immense difficulties faced today by the humanities in general and by state universities in particular. This edition could not have come to fruition without their support or without the administrative support of Margret Schluer, Ginnie Schmitz, and Derek Van Buskirk. I am indebted as well to Heather Hughes and Christine Thorsteinsson, at Harvard University Press, and to Melody Negron, at Westchester Publishing Services.

Research for this edition was conducted at the New York Public Library, the William Andrews Clark Memorial Library, the Harry Ransom Center, the Bodleian Library, and the British Library. The staffs at these libraries were unfailingly helpful, and I especially want to thank Scott Jacobs, Andrew Gantsky, and Kyle Tiplett for going to great lengths in helping me gather and access important materials.

Finally I offer my thanks to Merlin Holland, Wilde's grandson, not merely for the generosity with which he granted me permission to reproduce a part of Wilde's holograph manuscript, but also for the high benchmark set by his own scholarship, to which I, like all Wilde scholars, remain indebted.